Praise for Lauren Dane's *Standoff*

Rating: 5 Tattoos "Heavy tension keeps you on the edge of your seat from the first page of Standoff and refuses to let you go. The complex pack relations mixed with the burgeoning mate relationship between Cade and Grace make for some especially emotional moments as balance between pack and family is learnt by both."

~ *Erotic Escapades*

Rating: 4 ½ Stars "Lauren Dane has done a magnificent job of combining awesome characters and a sparkling plot. I only hope that this is not the last installment in the Cascadia Wolves series."

~ *JERR*

Rating: 5 Nymphs "I'll say up front that I loved this story. It has everything needed to make a great book...a well written and plotted ongoing storyline, great secondary characters well integrated from previous books and two sexy, determined and dedicated individuals as our hero and heroine. It's a thrilling story that pulled me in from the very first words and kept me racing through its pages until I reached the action filled end."

~ *Literary Nymphs*

Rating: “A” grade “I like the wolf characteristics that Dane keeps consistent with all of her characters even when they are in human form, including the submissive posture one takes when they’ve done wrong; the way they all have the need to touch, feel a touch, rubbing a cheek on a shoulder, a group hug when needed, and helping a wounded family member bring their wolf out to allow them to heal (this was done especially well in Wolf Unbound). Of course, all of the love scenes are sexy and hot. All the characters are paired perfectly, so anything from sex to teasing to raising their young is done exactly right.”

~ *The Good, The Bad, The Unread*

Look for these titles by

Lauren Dane

Now Available:

Reading Between The Lines

To Do List

Sweet Charity

Chase Brothers

Giving Chase

Taking Chase

Chased

Making Chase

Cascadia Wolves

Wolf Unbound

Standoff

Fated

Print Anthologies

Holiday Seduction

Cascadia Wolves: Standoff

Lauren Dane

A Samhain Publishing, Ltd. publication.

Samhain Publishing, Ltd.
577 Mulberry Street, Suite 1520
Macon, GA 31201
www.samhainpublishing.com

Standoff: Cascadia Wolves, Book 5

Print ISBN: 978-1-60504-095-0
Digital ISBN: 1-59998-884-4

Editing by Angela James
Cover by Anne Cain

First Samhain Publishing, Ltd. electronic publication: March 2008
First Samhain Publishing, Ltd. print publication: March 2009

Dedication

To Ann Leveille who encouraged me to write Enforcer after it had been rejected in another guise and started this whole journey.

To those readers who've ever so lovingly bugged me for Cade's story since the first book was published—this one is for you—as long as you don't break him, Grace is willing to share.

Angie James who I joke about—but in truth she's a rock star.

Ray, because no book would be complete without thanking the person who makes me believe in romance and happily ever after.

Chapter One

"What is this?"

The low-level Pack member tried to shut his laptop but Grace reached out and held it open, reading the screen. Her skin crawled as she saw the data there.

"I thought I said this wasn't to be tested."

The wolf had the good sense to look down. "Warren told me to pass the reports on to the lab down in Nashville."

Her jaw locked and she took a deep breath. Now wasn't the time to lose it or call attention to herself.

"Fine. But you need to CC me on everything. How can I do effective research if I don't know everything going on? This sort of thing, people doing all this around me and messing with the stream of data could set us back. I hardly think that's what your Alpha wants." Alpha, ha, that was laughable.

"Of course, Grace. I apologize."

Still, she knew none of them would do anything Warren didn't authorize. She pulled a phone from the pocket of her lab coat and called Warren Pellini's personal number.

"Warren, it's Grace. Look you need to be sure that when you're having the data sent elsewhere, I'm alerted."

"I thought you didn't want that data used. I wanted it to be sent where it might be seen with different eyes." His voice was cold.

She sighed her impatience. She didn't need to fake that. "Look, you brought me back to do this research. If you go around me and all sorts of data gets mixed from the different formulas and I don't know it, how can I make any accurate predictions of efficacy? All this stuff just floating out there from Pack to Pack. It's not secure, you don't know who's doing it under what control situations. I'm the doctor here, Warren, and I have the expertise you need. Let me do my damned job or don't waste my time."

He paused and she wondered for a bit if she hadn't overplayed her hand but after a time he cleared his throat. "Very well. You'll be alerted. I want the Nashville lab to have that data. We have some subjects down there I'm told are perfect for trials. You have full access, Grace, don't disappoint me." Nausea threatened at what she knew would happen to the homeless humans the Pack would use.

The call ended and within moments the wolf at the terminal got a message. A second after that he turned to her and nodded.

She needed to move and soon. Just another few days until she got more information and she'd get out. She couldn't risk it much longer without actively helping them or really exposing herself.

Warren's spies were everywhere, she trusted absolutely no one, not even her own parents. She just had to hold it together, every day, until she got home. Then she could turn on the shower and weep. Let the terror sweep through her until she had nothing left to cry with and managed to stumble into bed where fitful nightmares kept her awake.

So she could come back the next day, mask firmly in place, to play his fucked-up game and take him down. It had to happen and she would do what she had to. When she'd seen that first body come through her emergency room seven months earlier, she'd known Warren was responsible for it. Even if no one else in her Pack or her family knew right from wrong, Grace did. She hadn't left the *Group* and headed to medical school to pledge her life to helping people so Warren Pellini could unleash biological warfare on wolf and human alike. He had to be stopped.

It hadn't been easy to get back in touch. She'd had to earn his trust again but his ridiculous ego had been her best weapon in the end. He couldn't believe anyone would truly ever want to leave him, so within three months she'd gotten back into his good graces enough to get access to his labs. At least at one level. Since he'd killed several of his people in a fit of anger after the whole debacle with the Great Lakes Enforcer and the Cascadia people, she'd been far more important to him. Which put her a lot closer to the information she needed

Now she had access to the information which would eventually, or hopefully, bring him down. She just had to take it little by little in dribs and drabs. And hope no one caught her because if they did, who she was wouldn't save her.

"I don't need your permission, Lex. If you recall, *I'm* the Alpha here. So, well, that means what I say goes. It's pretty cool when you think about it." Cade Warden crossed his arms over his chest and glared at his brother, who crossed his arms and glared back.

"I'm aware of that, Cade. I'm your Enforcer. Your Second, which means I'm your advisor. Especially on issues of safety. You going to Chicago right now isn't safe. It's not advisable at all. There's a war, remember?"

"Yes. As a matter of fact I do. If *you* recall, I'm the one who declared it."

"Oh. My. God." Nina Warden, Lex's mate, stepped into the fray. "Cade, Lex is just watching out for your well-being."

"Nina, this doesn't concern you. I'm not having this discussion any further. It has to happen. Not only is Tegan tied up in knots over Ben taking this position in Great Lakes, but this new FBI task force needs to be sorted out. I'm not just going to let all this go on around me while I stay here."

"This does so concern me!"

Cade turned to where his sister-in-law lay propped in bed. "Nina, I love you so I usually let you have a lot of leeway in most things. Add to that, you're often right. But right now, you're supposed to be on your back in bed so you don't lose your damned pregnancy and Lex is needed *here.* I'm needed in Chicago."

"I am in bed. It's just as easy to needle you from here. Cade, it's so dangerous right now. Just do a conference call." He heard the anxiety in her voice.

"Are you saying my sister isn't worth a hug and some reassurance after she's given her entire life to this Pack?"

She winced and Cade felt bad for a moment but it needed to be said.

"You know I don't think that."

"Then let me go and stop making me feel guilty about it. Tegan needs me. She's my sister and one of my wolves. And my people need me to be active right now. The humans are pissed off and Ben can't handle it all. He's only been a wolf for less than a month."

"Cade." Lex paused and heaved a sigh. "Don't do this. I

don't want to leave Nina right now."

Cade relaxed and squeezed his brother's shoulder. "Don't leave her. That's an order. I'm Alpha, Lex. I may not have been an Army Ranger or be used as a cautionary tale to scare young wolves into staying out of trouble, but I am perfectly capable of protecting myself. Assign me a detail, include Dave or Megan but keep the others here with you. I'm leaving in three hours." He turned to Nina. "And you. You stay your ass in bed. Your doctor says you'll be okay in a week or so if you're *as still as possible* so shut up and be still."

Without another word, he left the room.

He phoned his parents, who supported his travel to Chicago, both as their son and as their Alpha. Megan had packed him a bag while he'd been in the shower and he made his goodbyes quick. Lex still glowered but his place was with Nina. The first week of pregnancy for a human transformed into a wolf was a dangerous time and it was necessary she be on bed rest. So it was necessary for Lex to be there to keep her in line. No one else could.

Cade was fucking sick of safety. He was a fucking Alpha. He'd been stuck there while Tegan had been kidnapped and tortured. It was Lex who went. Damn it, his family needed him. His freaking people needed him and he was going.

Megan brought two other wolves from the Enforcer corps, including Dave upon Lex's insistence. Cade trusted her, and them with his life. They drove to the airport in silence and loaded onto their private jet. It was quiet, near midnight and most everyone settled in to sleep for the flight.

Cade stretched out in the seat and looked out the window.

Megan came and snuggled into his side. "Hi," she whispered. "You okay?"

He smiled. It was just the two of them now. Alone and

unmated. He knew she'd started to get a bit restless but he'd been waiting the longest. At forty-two, he was more than ready to find his woman and start a family. He wanted what Lex and Nina had. Wanted what Tracy had with her mates. He wanted a woman to look at him the way Tegan looked at Ben. For two years he'd been anchored to Nina and felt deeply for her. She was like his mate, except they didn't share the most important thing, the utter intimacy she shared with Lex. She wasn't his. He wanted someone who was. Wanted to stop living off the echoes of someone else's relationship and have one of his own.

"I'm good. Tired. Worried about Tee. Are you okay with her moving?" Tegan was Megan's twin. The two were both on his guard detail. For many years after Tegan lost her first mate, she'd been a shadow and they'd just gotten her back only to lose her again to the distance between Seattle and Chicago.

"What else does she have? What other options does Ben have? He was put on leave after he was changed. He can't be a cop here anymore. His mother has disowned him. He's such a powerful wolf now, where would he fit in Cascadia?"

Ben Stoner, a cop and former human, had been transformed into a werewolf by a bite from the Alpha of the National Pack. The strongest wolf in the country. As wolves carried the traits of their sire if they were made, he was formidable. And there wasn't a place for him in Cascadia unless he challenged Lex, or Cade himself. And Ben wouldn't do that because he loved Tegan and he respected his brothers-in-law and the Cascadia wolves too much.

But it left Ben without a Pack, without a place and as war had been declared against the Pellini Group and all their affiliated Packs, all strong wolves needed to be in play. Ben needed to take on the Second position in Great Lakes, the largest and most powerful Pack in the United States. He belonged there and Tegan belonged there too.

It tore Cade apart. He loved his sisters and he'd lost two of them to other Packs in recent years. Tracy to Pacific but that was just in Portland and now Tegan to Chicago. He wanted to make things all right for the people he loved and so he'd go to Chicago and make sure Tegan understood he supported her in this move.

He nodded and put his arm around Megan's shoulders. "I'm going to miss her."

"Chicago isn't so very far away when you own a jet. Good thing you have that fancy business degree and have made Cascadia so rich. I can fly out and see her and we can go shopping. After the war is over. I don't imagine Ben is going to be up for her flitting around to shoe shop just now."

Cade laughed. "Poor Ben. Tee seems so mellow on the outside. She's not all hard-edged like Nina or even Tracy. But her will is ten thousand times more stubborn. I don't imagine Ben can stop her from doing whatever she wanted."

"Do you want to..." she paused, "...find someone? Have that? What they all have?"

"I do. So much I can't see straight. The older I get the worse it is. The lonelier it is."

She nodded. "I do too."

"I wish I could just wave a wand and fix it for us both. But Grandma got on the phone when I was talking to Mom and Dad earlier and she said a storm was coming. I'm guessing the mate thing will be on hold until after the war ends. So I hope that will be fast."

Ben and Tegan were there to meet their plane. Tegan looked better than he'd expected her to, given how badly she'd been injured just two weeks before.

His sister, long so closed off emotionally to everyone but her inner grief, saw him and smiled as she moved to him with her arms open. He hadn't seen her this open and happy in four years.

"Hey, Tee." He hugged her tight, fiercely pleased she'd greeted him so affectionately. When they broke the hug he took in Ben Stoner the werewolf, and saw Lex had been right about how powerful their brother-in-law had become after his change.

They clasped forearms as Megan and Tegan hugged and chatted. Their guards spread out to keep watch, mirroring Ben's team. And clearly they were Ben's. Attuned to him as he moved, adjusting themselves accordingly. Cade approved.

"Nicely done, Ben." Cade indicated the guards with a tip of his chin.

Ben smiled. "Thanks. It feels right. Come on, we've got you and your people set up in our house."

They loaded into several dark-windowed SUVs and headed away from the airport toward the Great Lakes compound.

"Are you sure your little cottage is going to fit us all?" Megan asked. She'd been there right after Tegan was found and had recovered.

"Maxwell gave us one of the houses about two miles from the Pack house. It's plenty large. Six bedrooms and plenty of bathrooms," Tegan explained. "We just moved in yesterday so things are a bit chaotic still. But the beds were delivered today and we even managed to get bedding put on them. And of course between me and Ben, the place is a fortress."

"They must have really wanted you to stay." Cade sat in the back with Ben. He could see Ben's fingers itching to take the wheel but he'd have to get used to it. He was important in an important Pack during wartime. It drove Cade crazy too.

Ben didn't speak loudly, he must have known Tegan would hear either way but he replied without taking his eyes from the back of her head. "Yes, I believe they do. I wish there was a way for me to fit at Cascadia. For her sake more than anything else. Hell, I wish I could have stayed on at the police department but I didn't take advice and told them about my change and suddenly I was on a health leave. I hope this isn't going to cause a problem between me and the rest of the family. I love Tegan, I want what's best for her. They've made her my Second, opened the Pack to both of us."

Cade heaved a breath. "There was no place for you, Ben. We all know that. I'm truly glad you've found such a good position. You'll keep her safe. Or safer anyway. And we're at war, we need every good soldier we can get. You bring a lot to us. Whether it's in Chicago or in Seattle, you're working and that's what counts."

They went through a series of checkpoints to get into the main heart of the compound.

"We've had a few attempts to breach security lately, I've stepped things up. There are multiple, manned checkpoints as well as remote sensors and constant patrols through the grounds." Ben got out when the car stopped and scanned the area before stepping aside for Cade.

"Come on inside. I've got dinner made." Tegan's eyes darted as she took in her surroundings, her hand at her hip where Cade knew she carried a weapon. Megan did the same, as did a host of other wolves.

"Damn, this place is huge. I visited the Pack house some years ago, before I became Alpha actually. This place gives it a run for its money." Cade walked inside and nodded to one of his men who went to take his bags to the room where Cade would be staying.

"Come on and eat. We have a meeting with Benoit tomorrow and there's been a new development I want to talk with you about." Ben guided them through the house and into the dining room.

"Would you like to clean up first?" Tegan stopped Cade with a hand on his arm. "Your room is at the top of the stairs, first door on the right."

"I'm good, Tee. Thanks. I'm starved though."

"Good, I made ribs. They've been marinating all day. With your sauce. Makes it feel like home." Her voice wasn't sad though. Cade relaxed at the sound. She was settled, happy. With all they faced, the last thing he wanted for anyone he loved was pain or sadness.

Once they'd finished the initial rush on the food, Ben sat back and grinned at Tegan. "That was amazing. Thank you."

She winked at him. "You can thank me later."

"Ew." Megan snorted. "Can one of your people show me the run of the place so I can get our team staged?"

Tegan excused herself to go and give the guards from Cascadia a tour.

"We got a call today. There's an insider from Pellini who wants to come in and talk to us. Tomorrow we'll talk about the task force with Benoit. He's working out of the Chicago field office for now. And this insider will come in to meet with us on Wednesday. Jack Meyers is coming in before the meeting to represent National." Ben sipped his wine.

"Who is it?"

"We don't know. Not for sure. The call was made from a disposable cell phone. Female, we know that. She says she's got info on the lab experiments but she couldn't get into detail. She was being watched. I'm a pretty good judge of character. She's scared but I didn't get the sense she was lying. Still, we're meeting in a secure location. Our people will pick her up and bring her in."

"We'll probably need to offer her safe passage, don't you think?" Cade pinched his bottom lip between his fingers a moment as he thought.

"If she's been exposed, yes. There's no way she'll be safe. We've seen what Pellini does to people he's displeased with. If not, if there's a way we can keep her inside as a mole." Ben shrugged. "We'd be crazy not to."

Cade exhaled. God, he was tired, so tired of always thinking about everyone else. Of always being in charge of everyone's safety and feelings. It came to him naturally, he was born to do it and he did it well, but at that moment, as he worried over the fate of some wolf he'd never even met, the burden crushed him.

Ben hesitated a moment before speaking again. "Cade, are you all right? Can I help in some way? I know I'm not Lex, I expect he's shouldering a lot too since war has been declared. I...it's just now that I'm a wolf, I feel so connected to everyone. Here at Great Lakes, I feel every wolf below me as a responsibility. I can't imagine what it's like for you. Every day, year after year. I know you do a good job, God knows I hear it all the time about you and Lex being so good at your jobs and all. Sometimes though...sometimes you might want a bit of help so you can breathe. If and when, I'm here. We're family."

"I keep forgetting you're a cop. You have a cop's way of seeing. I'm all right. It's good you're here. It's good I know Tegan is mated and happy and has found a place with you. Having to tell you to stay away from Cascadia gatherings until you'd chosen a place in a Pack was difficult. I don't want my sister or you to ever feel slighted by your own family."

Ben shrugged and leaned back in his chair. "I understand why you had to do it. So does Tegan. It was a potential powder keg with me unaffiliated like that. You had to protect the Pack at a time right after war had been declared. And as for being slighted by my own family, I have been. My sister still speaks to me but my parents have refused since I was changed."

Cade couldn't imagine what that must have felt like. The utter desolation and loss. "It's truly their loss, Ben. It's not the same, I know, but you're my brother and you're part of my family. You're ours now just as we're yours. Great Lakes or Cascadia, none of that matters."

Ben nodded. "Thanks. You want to motor up to the Pack house and do your Alpha thing with Maxwell?"

"I suppose that's what protocol demands." Cade stood. "Let me go and clean up. Get a new shirt. I'll be right back down."

Later, sometime long after midnight after he'd returned to Tegan and Ben's, he'd stood and looked at his reflection. After this damned war was finished, he was taking some time for himself. He'd been living half a life through his brother's mate bond and he was sick of yearning. Sick of wanting what he couldn't have and never would.

At forty-two he'd never paused to feel sorry for himself or to allow this sort of maudlin shit in his life. He had a job. A calling. To be an Alpha was a special gift. Only one wolf could hold that spot in a Pack. It was more than strength and intelligence, it was a combination of charisma, savvy, and political astuteness that all worked together and created one wolf they all looked to. One wolf who held their hearts, their joy and pain, their will and destiny in his hands. To be an Alpha was only a dream to all but a tiny minority and he was honored he'd been born and chosen to lead. He loved his wolves.

At the same time a deepening emptiness had stolen into his soul and with each passing day, it grew colder and colder. The last two years, watching Lex with Nina, seeing the completeness it brought to his brother's life, satisfied him but ate away at him too. Cade didn't want to be petty or avaricious. How could he begrudge Tegan this happiness she'd found? Or Tracy?

And yet, he wanted it too and it wasn't too much to ask. There hadn't been time for him to fully search for a mate but this war would end one way or another and when it did, he would find her or die trying before the emptiness swallowed him whole.

Chapter Two

The next day they headed up to the Pack house for the task force meeting. Benoit agreed to come out there rather than have the wolves meet him at the field office. Security would have been a nightmare and many of the human FBI agents didn't trust the wolves. Especially after Benoit had been nearly killed when Pellini attacked the Palaver. Complicating matters further, Benoit's former assistant, a werewolf, had resigned and gone back to his own Pack when war had been declared.

Guards constantly patrolled the grounds and Tegan wore an earpiece, keeping in contact at all times. National's guards worked in teams with those Tegan ran in Ben's name. Cade had asked why she didn't take the position of Enforcer along with Ben. His sister had replied that she had, but in her own way, which was to provide on the ground support to Ben who'd fill the strategic spot. The two of them created one perfect working unit. Cade saw it in action. Watched as each of them did their part and created a peerless team.

A quiet bit of movement and speaking into wrist mics and the car carrying Benoit and another human agent approached the house. They got out and the hand shaking and basic posturing took up another five minutes until Ben and his friend finally laughed and entered the house together.

"We've set up for several calls and some tele-conferencing in the main room," Tegan told them as she arrived with a smile for Benoit.

Once all the Alphas and Enforcers in their Alliance had gotten on the line or connected via computer screen, they got started.

Cade, as the Alpha who'd declared war initially, took the meeting in hand. Ben and Lex had both briefed him thoroughly and he'd studied everything Jack brought. It hadn't been a pretty picture.

"I'm just going to cut through all the bullshit here and get to the point. There have been more bodies. This time in Rhode Island. Adding the number to Nashville, here and New Orleans, we've got a total of forty-eight. I hope, Agent Benoit, you'll keep this as confidential as possible, but we have every reason to believe this is related to Warren Pellini."

"What makes you think so?" Benoit made direct eye contact with Cade and held it.

"They're partially transformed. Caught between human and wolf. Some burned, some disfigured with chemicals. He did the same thing here for some months. Given the state of the lab we busted a little over two weeks back, Pellini has some nasty tech up his sleeve."

The crack in Benoit's jaw sounded as he tightened. His anger radiated and every wolf in the room scented it. They'd expected it. Benoit had no real idea just how much they hadn't shared.

"And you didn't feel it was necessary to share this information with us until now, why?" Caldwell, the other agent with Benoit asked.

"Until recently, we'd deemed this a Pack issue, best handled between wolves." Cade would not apologize for putting his people first.

"Bullshit. Why now then? Why tell us now?" Benoit's anger remained like a bitter stink.

"The bodies are racking up. We can't ignore it. If we didn't come to you now, if we didn't agree to this task force, we'd be placing our people in more danger. Our people aren't the threat, Pellini's people are."

"And we don't want humans to be targeted or to target us either," Ben smoothly interrupted Cade. "Look, I know you're pissed. And you have a right to be. But all we can do from this point is to move forward. We won't be sharing everything, we can't and it's not necessary. But as it concerns humans and anything that could harm human populations, we want to help."

"Start with this Declaration of War," Benoit said flatly.

Ben cut his eyes to Maxwell and then to Cade, who sighed and nodded. Best to just cede this to Ben as he had the closest tie with the FBI at that point.

"When Pellini came into that meeting and attacked people, he broke a very old law. Palaver, or that type of cross Pack meeting is sacred. Everyone involved has been granted safe passage. By killing wolves there, by attacking, he's made himself an outlaw. More than that, he attacked and nearly killed Tegan, a highly placed Cascadia wolf and the Enforcer of the strongest Pack in the US. War was declared against Pellini and any Pack who affiliates or aligns with them." Now it was Ben's anger that clung to the back of Cade's throat.

He carefully filled them in on what had been happening without going too deeply into details. Cade knew it had to be difficult for Ben; the man was a cop, he'd want to deal honestly with the authorities and in this case, this was *Pack business* and not the concern of humans.

"Here's what's going to happen. There will be a task force. Human authorities, as in us at the FBI and some key local law enforcement and wolves of your choosing. I'd like to request Ben and Lex because I've worked with both men and trust them both with my life. We'll need to be kept abreast of things. No more bullshit secrets. I'm willing to keep as much of this war crap out of my report as I can, but in return, I expect to be informed." Benoit sat back in his chair and challenged them to argue.

Cade didn't and neither did Maxwell. It was a good deal.

"Ben, looks like you've got another job," Maxwell said with a shrug.

"Lex, I trust you'll get in touch with Agent Benoit?" Cade hadn't told anyone of Nina's pregnancy just yet. She didn't want anyone to worry and she'd tell everyone herself in a week when she got the all clear.

"Right. And Cade, you and I need to speak when you're finished there." Lex's voice was tight. Cade knew how he must be itching to know everything, to control what was happening from afar. It was almost amusing, thinking of how his brother must be dancing around in his seat.

Almost.

They set up a time for the next conference call and Benoit and Caldwell were escorted to the front gates after Ben had a quiet conversation with them at their car.

He came back in just a few minutes later and sat. Now it was on to wolf business.

"Ben and Tee, I want to congratulate you both. I wish...well, I wish we could have made a comfortable place for you here but I know you'll do a great job with Great Lakes. Don't let Tegan rip the heads off anyone though, those redheaded sisters of mine have hair-trigger tempers," Lex said.

Tegan snorted quietly and Cade heard Nina snicker in the background.

"Things are what they are. It's the way it's supposed to be." Tegan spoke from her perch across the table.

Ben filled everyone in on the new information and the possible informant. He didn't give any specifics, although they knew they could trust every wolf on the line, they didn't want to take a chance with such a sensitive subject.

"Now that the humans are gone, I need to report some border skirmishes. Pellini-allied wolves from Yellowstone ambushed four Grand Teton Pack members, including a child," Jack Meyers interrupted.

A wave of outrage, sharp like stinging rain, blanketed the room. Harming children? What was next?

"This is quick for posturing, isn't it?" Maxwell rubbed his chin. "If war is what Warren Pellini wants, he'll have it rammed right down his fucking throat."

"What's the history anyway? Between you and Pellini?" Ben asked, after checking in with his people.

"Warren Pellini was one of my wolves. Not very high ranked. He was shunned, took several wolves with him and set up his *group* just outside my main territory. His family mainly but other rogues showed up. They didn't do much at first so we ignored them. He wasn't worth my effort, or so I thought. And by the time I realized he was, he'd gone underground. There's a bounty on his head as a feral wolf in my region. I should have killed him right off." Maxwell sighed. "He was an idiot. I was glad to be rid of him and his crazy ideas. I hadn't anticipated he'd set up an organized crime syndicate. And by the time it came out and I got wind of it, he'd moved around so much and kept low so I couldn't find him."

"Hindsight." Cade raised one eyebrow at the other Alpha.

"Too late for recriminations. We push forward because there's nothing to be gained in looking back. He's dead. Period. Harming children is just another reason, but we've had reason enough for some time. The moment he put silver in my sister, he signed his death warrant." Violence fueled Cade's rage like a furnace. Heat suffused him, he clenched his fists, wishing Pellini was right there so he could rip him from limb to limb himself.

When he looked up, he saw approval and a mirror of his rage in Ben's eyes.

The Council of War continued to meet, shoring up border regions, stepping up defenses and preparing for any offensive actions that would come soon enough.

"All right, we're alone, what's up? Nina okay?" Cade settled in on the phone in his room back at Tegan's to receive a lecture from Lex.

"What's this about a special meeting tomorrow? Are you secure enough? Why is it offsite?"

"Lex, let me introduce myself. I'm Cade Warden, I've been the Alpha of the Cascadia Wolf Pack for twelve years. I'm no wet behind the ears cub. And Ben is no slouch with security. The informant is coming. I want to meet her myself."

"I don't like this one bit."

"I know you don't. You want to be here and you can't, so deal with that. You have other responsibilities. Nina comes first. By the way, you're the best Enforcer there is, but not the only one. I have four of my own guard and there are plenty here as well. I'll call you when it's over."

"No one can handle it as well as I could. I don't trust your safety to anyone else."

"I'll tell Tegan you said that, shall I?" Cade shoved his annoyance away. It wasn't the time for a sibling spat with his brother. "Look, Lex, I know you're concerned and I appreciate it but everyone seems to forget I'm Alpha for a reason. I can handle myself. On top of that, Ben and Tegan run a tight ship." Cade told Lex all about how the two of them seemed to form one airtight security machine.

"Damn. Is that as scary as it sounds?" Lex laughed.

"It is. Now, I'm going to bed. Give your wife a kiss for me and I'll talk to you tomorrow afternoon when I finish up. I'll be home by the weekend. When I get back, I expect a full report on what we're doing to keep our wolves safe." Cade hung up moments later and went downstairs to spend some time with his sisters.

Chapter Three

Grace tried not to fidget as she sat at the park bench near the bus stop. They'd told her to wait there for instructions. She was pretty sure Warren's people hadn't followed her. Pretty sure. All she had was hope at that point.

A man sat next to her, putting a book down between them and leaning forward. It was titled *The Source*. At second sniff, the man wasn't a man but a wolf and not a Pellini wolf.

Picking the book up, she opened it to the bookmarked page. *Follow me and get in the car. Don't look back.*

An SUV with dark windows slid up and the door opened. Grace followed the man and got in, shutting the door behind her.

"We're on the way to the meeting now. Are you wearing any device that could be a tracker?" The man turned to her. Blue-gray eyes took her in from head to toe. Handsome, this wolf, but violence emanated from him as well. She wondered if he blamed her for the insanity her brother spread like a disease.

"I-I don't think so."

"My name is Ben Stoner. We're going to stop and check you over first and then we'll get to the meeting. You have nothing to fear from us unless you bring it on yourself." He sat back quietly until they reached a warehouse and drove up and inside.

"Out now please." He held the door open and steadied her with a helping hand. "Wand her."

"Don't you want my name?" Grace asked in what she hoped was a calm voice.

"No. Not yet. Save it for the meeting. Do you have weapons?"

"No!"

"Hey, don't get offended. I'm taking you into a meeting with important people, I can't let you walk in there packing. It's sort of my job and all."

"And my kind isn't trustworthy?" She knew it sounded petulant but she was risking her life for them.

"I don't know shit about your kind. I only know about Warren Pellini and his kind. If you're his kind, no, you're not trustworthy. But it seems to me, if you're on the level, you're risking a lot and you're not his kind."

"Oh. Well. I apologize for snapping at you." She smoothed a hand down her skirt nervously.

He laughed. "I imagine you're nervous. Now, my people say you're clean so let's go. One warning, no sudden moves when we arrive. All my people have shoot-to-kill orders. That's my family in there, I won't let you harm them. Understood?"

She nodded.

Two more SUVs joined them, one in front and the other behind. They entered several checkpoints and moved through gates and behind walls until they stopped in front of an ivy-covered house.

No mistaking the state of war though. Wolf guards patrolled every few feet carrying large, scary weapons and looking tightly wired. What had she gotten herself into? Rhetorical of course. Her brother may be a soulless murderer but she wasn't. It was her responsibility to help.

"Let's go then. Remember, no sudden moves, all right?"

Gulping and swallowing nothing but dust, she followed him into the building, surrounded by guards.

And when she entered the large dining room, dominated by a large table, in turn dominated by wolves so powerful the air vibrated with it, she nearly lost her knees as she locked eyes with the hazel-eyed male near the head.

Never had she seen a more incredibly alluring male. Strong. His power, quiet and confident, rolled from him and caressed her. She sent out silent thanks she was wearing a padded bra or everyone would have known just how she was being caressed. It wouldn't protect her from their sensitive noses though as her pussy softened and readied for him alone. Christ, what was this? Some sort of odd adrenaline response to her fear and nervousness?

Cade turned up to get a look at their informant. Tegan had let them know the convoy arrived and they were on their way inside.

His gut did a freefall. She'd be a honey-colored wolf. Slight, petite even. Graceful though. Her hair hung in a straight curtain to her shoulders, smooth. Smooth like the creamy skin over high cheekbones. Lush lips. Big, scared brown eyes. She couldn't have been more than barely five feet and an inch or two, even in her sensible heels. Her legs were bare beneath the skirt that skimmed just below her knees. The dark blue of the blouse didn't do much for her coloring.

Without thinking, he stood and the room went silent. Megan moved to his side, ready to leap or do whatever he needed. Tegan flanked his other side and Ben moved to stand next to the woman.

"Who are you?" Cade asked.

"Grace. Grace Pellini. I have information for you." Her voice, what was it about her voice? So soft, comforting. It wasn't as if she whispered, but still, so soft, so pretty.

"Please, please sit down and talk to us." Cade indicated the place just across from him and she sat, her eyes not moving from his.

"I'm Cade Warden, Alpha of Cascadia. This is Maxwell Williams, Alpha of Great Lakes." Cade continued to introduce the major players but it was as if he said it on auto pilot as he struggled to get over the need to touch her.

"I know who Maxwell is." Her mouth canted down for a moment before she seemed to mentally wave it away and focus back on him. "Alpha of Cascadia. My brother tried to kill your sister a little over two weeks ago."

He scented her anxiety and wanted to fix it. The need to make her feel better made his head swim.

"Did you try to help him?"

The shock on her face answered his question. "No. I'd never. No. I wasn't allowed in that part of the lab complex. But one of my, well, one of the wolves I trusted more than the others, not totally of course, he helped her, didn't he?"

"Yes. One of the Pellini wolves kept me sedated and tried to protect me the best he could. He's safe now. I'm Tegan, Cade's sister and Second here at Great Lakes along with my mate, Ben."

"Grace, tell us what you came here to say and why we should believe you." Jack Meyers, a man who pulled no punches, said what needed to be said but it did annoy Cade on some level.

Still, the woman seemed to be made of sterner stuff and

looked unruffled by Jack's straightforward question. "When Warren was shunned and left Great Lakes to start his own Pack, I was in medical school. I lost my status here with Great Lakes just like the rest of my family did." Her eyes cut to Maxwell briefly. "I had no Pack but for what Warren created. But I've never been close to my family. I've been estranged from them for several years but seven months back a body came through my emergency room and I smelled my brother on him. He'd—the victim—been partially transformed but his DNA wasn't all wolf or all human. It was broken. His entire system just sort of collapsed in on itself."

Cade pushed a glass of water her way and she sipped it before speaking again.

"I'd heard the rumor he'd...Warren...stolen a copy of the lycanthropy virus but I thought he'd lost it. That body in my ER said otherwise. So I went to him and said I wanted back in the family. I was alone, without a Pack, it wasn't so hard to believe really. After a while, I offered to help with my medical skills and he didn't trust me so he gave me nickel and dime stuff. But I did it and kept at it and the bodies showed up in my ER until I went nearly mad with the anger. I confronted him about it but pretended I was mad he was being so careless. That's when he let me in part way and I've been working my way closer and closer to this project ever since. When he lost the big lab two weeks ago after you rescued Tegan, he let me in even more because he lost a lot of data. But I don't know how much more I can get. He's suspicious and I can't hide how distressed I am with all this."

She reached into her pocket and tossed a small memory card on the table. "There's some data there. Not a lot because he's got the computers in the labs monitored very closely."

"Does he have the virus?" Cade asked.

"Not the full virus. What he has is partially correct. That's why he's been experimenting on the homeless humans. But he gets closer every week. What he used on the Enforcer he murdered was very close."

Maxwell leaned forward. "What?"

"It's not the complete virus. He had that once, back when he assassinated your Third two years ago. But he lost it then and apparently has spent the intervening time attempting to re-create it."

"No, not that. We know that, or suspected anyway. We didn't know what happened to Gina, our Enforcer. We never found her body. We'd heard he killed her but we didn't know how." Maxwell heaved a troubled sigh.

"Ah. Yes. He used a bastardized version on her and it killed her. I'm sorry for her and her family. I never met her of course, she came on after you so unceremoniously shunned my entire family from this Pack, but I'd never want an innocent to suffer for what the guilty did." Her eyes held Maxwell's, and Cade's wolf agitatedly pressed against his human skin.

"I did what I had to do. Warren was a cancer in this Pack."

"Yes. Well you must be so proud of the outcome." Grace cocked her head and glared at one of the most powerful wolves Cade had ever met. An amused smile dragged one corner of his mouth up. Gutsy, this wolf. "You had a responsibility to all your wolves and you tossed everyone in our family to the wind to punish my brother. It seems...unnecessarily overbroad. But what do I know? I've been without a Pack for years now because it was my criminally insane brother or nothing so I chose nothing."

Maxwell rubbed his face and sighed.

Tegan settled in just behind Cade, he felt her amusement. Cade wondered idly just what he'd have done in Maxwell's place. It seemed a bit of an overreaction to shun an entire family but having members in your Pack who were so openly criminal and destructive *was* a cancer. It ate away at morale. His brother-in-law Nick's Pack, Pacific, had a similar problem, only it had been at the top. Some years before, Cascadia had its own issues. It was Monday morning quarterbacking to try and second guess another Alpha in a situation like this one.

"Can you speak with some of our researchers about this?" Cade asked her. "We've got a lab, have had one for several years now. I'm sure they'd understand you far better than we can."

Those amber depths met his and settled in at the base of his spine.

"We can get you back to your location safely," Maxwell said.

Cade turned, a growl trickling from his lips. "We can't risk her now!"

"There's no reason to believe anyone saw her meeting with us, Cade." Maxwell's eyes widened a moment as they moved back and forth between Cade and Grace.

"Can you just so casually put her in danger this way? We know what he's capable of, Maxwell. Will you just throw her to the dogs because you're done with her? Just toss her back like you did the rest of her family?" Whoa, that was out of bounds. Cade knew it and yet, he couldn't quite stop the flow of anger driving his words.

"That's not fair, Cade," Tegan said quietly.

"No, he's got a point." Maxwell shrugged. "I did clearly make too broad a choice when I shunned Pellini's whole family. Grace was one of my wolves and I didn't do my duty by her or the others in Warren's family when I shunned them all. But I'm not just tossing her into danger unceremoniously because I don't care. I truly think she's been unexposed. Ben said so and I trust my Enforcer."

Without meaning to, Cade stood and moved to her. Alarmed, she'd stood as well, pushing her chair back, her stance mirroring his.

Things were moving fast, teetering on the edge of sliding out of control but Cade's wolf had taken over.

Cade breathed in to try and center himself and push his wolf back down. Instead, he got a gut full of her scent. He grabbed her hands and she swayed. His entire world rocked on its foundations and re-settled as he truly saw her for what she was.

Dimly in the background he heard Megan curse and felt her move back.

"Someone want to tell me what the hell is going on?" Ben asked. "Do we have trouble or what?"

Possessiveness and protectiveness nearly blinded Cade as he grabbed Grace around the waist and put himself between Ben and her with a snarl. Ben stood his ground, examining Cade's face.

"Not the kind of trouble you think." He turned to face Grace again. The fear on her face softened when he touched her cheek, wanting to calm her. "Thank God you're not his wife."

Shocked laughter exploded from her, strained at the edges.

"I'm not going to send you back. You know that, right?"

It couldn't be. What a freakish bit of irony that would be. Wouldn't it? She leaned toward him slowly, sure he'd protect her but remembering Ben's warning about moving slow. When she breathed him in, her wolf rushed to the surface, pushing at her human skin. An involuntary growl trickled from her lips and without intending to, she bit him where neck met shoulder and her pussy clenched, needing him there. Her body tightened, hardened, and softened all at once.

She'd heard stories about what it was to find your mate. Hadn't given them much credence because she lived outside a Pack for so long. She figured she'd find a human man, marry him, adopt kids and never live as a wolf again.

But there, with his flesh in her mouth, with his taste racing through her, imprinting her system, marking her in a way she was sure she'd never forget, she wanted to weep at the idea she'd been willing to give this up.

It was magic. Beautiful, soulful magic and what a tremendous gift. She'd have his babies, live at his side. Wake up with him and be his woman as he'd be her man. This beautiful, strong wolf who fit into her soul like a key in a lock.

His head dropped back as he pulled her against his body. "It's you." The wonder in his voice eased any worry she'd had that her feelings were one-sided.

Despite the utter ridiculousness of finding her mate in the greatest enemy of her family, she laughed, joy filling her. "It's me. Oh that fate, she's laughing right now."

Behind Cade, Ben laughed along with his beautiful, red-haired mate. "It seems all of us have given fate a great deal of amusement. I take it you've just met your mate, Cade?"

"Yes, I believe I have." Grace loved the way it seemed as if Cade couldn't stop touching her, running his hands up and down her arms, smiling. His scent, fully aroused male wolf, tickled her nose and brought her wolf to the surface. It had been so long that she'd allowed her other nature, her other half to surface in response to any strong emotion. In Cade Warden she hadn't just found a mate, she'd rediscovered herself.

Still, she needed him badly. Baldly. Her vision swam as pheromones pulsed through her body in response to his. His musk, his arousal, his need for her, his wolf calling to hers all set her firmly off balance. Her fingers dug into his upper arms to try and stay alert, to keep her knees when she wanted to rip off her clothes and impale herself on his cock.

A soft needy sound escaped her lips and his pupils swallowed his eyes. His cock, hard and ready, pressed against her belly. She needed him to fix it, make it better.

He'd finally found her.

Need. Need to claim her swept through him painfully even as the joy buffeted his heart. He needed to claim her, mark her, solidify their bond. Protect her.

"I need to..." she shook her head, "...please, Cade. Do you feel it too?"

Unable not to, he brushed his lips over hers, allowing what he thought was a small taste. He groaned at the music of her, of the delicacy and beauty of her against his lips. She seduced him, enchanted him. "I do, I do."

"Take me then, Cade. Mark me and make me yours." Her hands fisted in the front of his shirt, not wanting to let him go. The desperation in her voice echoed his own.

He was an Alpha wolf, there's no way he should have his control so challenged. And yet, his hands trembled, his muscles ached.

Megan touched his arm. "You have to. Go. Go and perform the bond. You've waited so long. You'll both be stronger for it."

Maxwell spoke from the table. "I agree. We all do. You've been given something special. We celebrate each and every time a mated pair comes together. Times seem bleak just now so let's all take our blessings when we can get them."

Ben handed him keys. "Three miles up the road. Bear right along the treeline. There's a little blue cottage. Go on. You need the time. You're safe here within the walls."

No other words were needed. Cade stood back and held his hand to Grace, she took it and let him draw her to the door. There wasn't anything else in the world then but her. Just her.

"Come on."

In the car, she stayed quiet, just looking at him, taking in every part of his face. She tried not to think about the way the need for him crawled over her skin. *Just a few minutes more*, she kept telling herself.

When they pulled into the driveway of the cottage, she yanked the door open before he could come around to get her. She'd let him open doors for her to his heart's content another day. For now, for now the urgency would reign until he filled her and marked her.

"Front door? Key?" She danced around like she had to use the bathroom.

He looked at her as he fumbled with the lock and laughed. "Hungry for my cock?"

Her breath caught and she blinked a few times at the visual he'd evoked with his naughty words. Since no words came, she just nodded earnestly.

The door opened and they tumbled through. He slammed it with a foot and locked it with one hand while the other yanked at her as his mouth descended to hers.

There was no holding back in his kiss. His tongue slipped into her mouth, demanding her response and she gave it. It wasn't that she didn't like sex, but no one had ever been so evocative before. She hadn't the time in residency and before she'd been very young and involved in school. Since then, there'd only been one person, a quick three week thing.

The desire that'd lay coiled, quiet inside her for years roared to life at his touch, at his taste. Heat flushed her skin, her nipples hardened to the point of pain, her clit grew sensitized and each step she walked, the slick flesh around it stroked her, making her nearly pant with need.

He pulled back from their kiss, slowly tugging on her bottom lip with his teeth. A sort of squeak of desperation came from her and he cocked his head.

"You need it bad, don't you?" His voice, low and growly, caressed her skin, making her arch. He traced the tendon from shoulder to ear with his tongue. "I find I like that very much, Grace."

"Can you like it while you're, while we're, you know, doing it?"

He backed her through the house, looking from side to side until he finally hummed his satisfaction and they entered a room with a bed.

"Doing it? Fucking you? Spreading you out beneath me and sliding my cock deep inside you? Is that what you mean?" He paused as he tossed her on the bed and went to work unbuttoning his shirt and getting rid of his tie.

His upper body was hard and muscled. A nice bit of hair on his chest and a thin arrow leading down into the waistband of his pants. She nearly gulped when she got a load of that flat, masculine stomach. She tried to speak but just shut her mouth when all she managed was a sort of strangled gasp.

His eyes caught her again. "Look at you. What a pretty woman you are, especially when you blush. Show me your body, Grace."

With shaking hands, she managed to get rid of her suit jacket and unmoored the buttons of her blouse, exposing the silk camisole beneath it.

"Oh, very, very sexy. That silk looks almost as good as your skin." Cade stood before her, gloriously naked, his eyes on her body.

She'd always felt like a boy, her breasts were small, for a wolf she was especially diminutive, just barely five feet two. Most of the time she wore a lab coat, sensible shoes and drab clothing. It wasn't like working in an emergency room had a whole lot of opportunity for glamour. But the way he looked at her made her feel beautiful in a way she'd never experienced before. She felt totally feminine and very sexy.

"You're blushing." He leaned down and caught her foot, easing off one shoe, catching the other foot and doing the same.

"You make me feel shy and wanton all at once."

"Let's work on wanton."

She helped him undo the zipper on her skirt and she watched, heart in her throat, as he tossed it behind him. Big hands slid up her calves, up her thighs until he hooked his fingertips in her very sensible cotton panties and pulled them down and off her legs.

"You never have to be shy with me. I'm yours. No judgment, only adoration. I've waited for you for what seems like forever." She watched, fascinated, as he pressed a kiss at her ankle, then another just higher.

"Are you all right?" he asked when she hadn't said anything.

She nodded, slowly. "I-I just..."

He surged up, pressing a kiss right on her pussy and she gasped as sensation flooded her. In another deft movement she could barely track it was so fast, he'd rolled onto the bed, bringing her astride him.

"Camisole off. I want to see your breasts. And you just

what?"

Instead of trying to explain how totally he overwhelmed her, she lifted up on her knees, reached around and guided the head of his cock, pressing down, taking him deep.

"Fuck!" He rolled his hips, thrusting into her. Without waiting for her to comply, he whipped the cami off and sucked in a breath.

She moved her hands to cover herself, blushing. But he growled, grasping her wrists and pulling her away.

"They're beautiful, don't hide them." He took her nipples between his fingers, pulling and twisting them until she ground herself against his pubic bone.

"They're small." She moved against him desperately.

He rolled again, this time on top of her. Grasping her ankles, he brought her legs up and apart. "Mmm, very limber. Nice. Now, let's get a few things straight right now, shall we?" He leaned down and took one of her nipples between his teeth.

She cried out as shards of white hot pleasure sliced through her. Her fingers tangled through his thick hair, holding him to her breast.

"Your cunt just rippled around my cock. Do you know why?" he asked, his eyes grabbing her gaze and holding her to his. She shook her head.

"Because you were made for me and I'm made for you. That's thing one." He pulled nearly all the way out and plunged back deep. "Thing two is that your breasts are fucking gorgeous. Perfect. Just what I've fantasized about and very sensitive. Thing three is that you started to tell me something and tried to avoid it by surrounding me with your very hot, very tight, very juicy pussy. And while I have no objections to being buried inside you, I do want you to always talk to me."

"Can you please get to the task?" It burst from her lips without meaning to. "Please!"

He laughed. "All right. But we're going to talk. Afterward."

But he pulled out and she grasped empty air as he moved down her body. "No! Not that right now!"

His mouth found her pussy and she closed her eyes a moment. She couldn't help it, it felt so damned good. But she didn't want that right then. She needed him to spill his damned semen inside her and seal the bond. Her body knew it.

"I need to see you come first. Then I'll fuck you and claim you. I promise." He went back to work and she punched the mattress as he chuckled.

Cade thought he'd come when her honey made contact with his tongue. Christ, she tasted good. She'd protested at first but as he flicked his tongue over her juicy little clit she began to make tiny, breathy sounds as her fingers dug into the blankets beneath them.

The shy thing did something to him. He wasn't sure why, he'd usually sought out bolder women. It was just her, the way she looked, the way she fit against him, the taste of her skin. Her cunt was so tight he'd been afraid to hurt her but when she wanted it bad enough, she got bold and demanded it. He liked that too.

His fingers delved into her pussy while he held her to his mouth, devouring her. Her honey rained on his lips when she gasped and arched. His name on her lips shot triumph through his system as she came.

Moving quickly, he flipped her over and entered her from behind. The way she pushed back against him told him she liked it this way too. Good. The curve of her spine, the delicate bumps of each vertebrae, drove his wolf wild.

"Harder," she gasped into the pillow.

"Hmm, not as shy as I thought," he murmured, quite happy to oblige her request.

Her cunt grabbed his cock in such a tight embrace he wasn't sure how long he'd be able to make it last. So good, she felt so good he never wanted it to end, and yet, his balls drew up tightly against his body and the need to come began to pound in his ears, coursing through his veins.

She writhed, the honeyed gold of her hair sliding to the side to give him coy glances of her face. He caught the sight of her bottom lip between her teeth, her eyes closed, long lashes fanned against her pale skin.

She had to be there with him, had to come when he did. He reached around to slide his fingers through her pussy, up to find her clit. A surprised moan vibrated through her as she jerked forward into his touch.

"Mmm, you like that."

She mumbled something into the pillow and he laughed even as his cock ached.

"Come with me, beautiful."

At that moment, her inner walls rippled and spasmed as she came. He heard his name whispering from her lips. The sound, the rightness of it, coupled with the way she felt around him brought his climax with blinding intensity.

One last thrust deep into her body and he was lost to the pleasure.

Chapter Four

Grace felt him push deep and his cock jerked within her body as he came. His hands gripped her hips, held her and her body moved with the last remnants of her own orgasm.

And dimly she realized he'd moved to the side when the tide of the bond yanked her under. Pulled her down to where all she knew was the crush of emotions so intense she lost herself for long moments as she sweated and trembled.

Her body ached, hurt and yet, even as it spiraled out of her grasp, it began to re-work, her system rebuilding itself back with his, his DNA morphing hers into something new.

Suddenly, it clicked into place and she gasped, sitting up.

His arms held her, he rocked her back and forth, his lips against her temple whispering softly.

"Honey? Are you all right?"

She not only heard the angst and worry in his voice, she felt it through their link. When she opened her eyes, she met his hazel ones and felt better than she ever had.

"Yes, yes, I'm fine now." Reaching up, she pushed a lock of his hair out of his face. "You're so gorgeous. I've never seen anyone as handsome as you are."

"Thank you, honey. I feel the same way about you. Everything in the universe is totally fucked up but for the first time in my entire life I am completely at ease. Satisfied. Full and proud. I've waited so long for you I began to wonder if you were just a figment of my imagination."

A sob tore from her and she buried her face in his chest, breathing him in. She felt his alarm through their link.

"Grace? What is it?"

How could she explain it? How alone she'd been in the world? She shook her head and he stroked a hand over her hair. He was so damned big and she'd been afraid for so long she didn't know what to do with the absence of both the fear and the loneliness.

"Tell me, please. How can I help if you don't tell me?"

"It's just...I don't know how to say it and not sound pathetic. I'm not."

He drew her away from his chest with such infinite patience and gentleness, it shook her. "I don't think you're pathetic, Grace. But what I do know is you can trust me with your heart, with your soul."

"I've been alone for a very long time. I've had friends, of course, human friends. But when Maxwell shunned Warren, none of the rest of the Pack were allowed to speak to us. I lost everyone. And then of course, I drew away from Warren and the rest of his *group* because they're all horrible, including my parents. Now I have you and it feels so wonderful I guess it just was very apparent, how alone I really was when I didn't feel it anymore."

Her voice became more and more sure as she spoke, as she realized it was all right to share her feelings with him.

"Since I've been back with him to get this information, I've been scared. So damned scared that he'd find out what I was up to and hurt me. Use that virus on me. What he did to Gina, what he's done to those homeless humans, it's barbaric."

"You aren't going back. You can't. You'll be marked with my scent as my mate. He'd know and there's no way in hell I'd let you be endangered like that. Ever. Know that, Grace. I'd give my life for you and Maxwell can hang if he thinks anything else."

He kissed her, hard at first and then softer. "My Pack is your family now. My family is yours. No more being alone. You have me and five of my siblings. All of them but one have mated. My sister Layla has two kids and Nina, my other sister-in-law and my anchor bond is pregnant. My parents are alive as is my grandmother. Lots of family to love you, and they will. Oh, and Tracy, my youngest sibling has a three-legged dog who isn't all there. Don't ask." He laughed.

Blech, anchor bond? She'd have to face that herself soon enough, she really didn't want to think about some other woman being his anchor.

"I'd be perfectly happy to never deal with Warren or Maxwell again. Both of them are assholes. Warren is worse, but Maxwell's actions put many wolves in this position."

Cade loved the tilt of her chin when she finally got her mad on. She was little but had a heck of a spark.

"I can't know for sure what I'd have done in Maxwell's place, but I'm on your side here. He shouldn't have shunned you all that way. But you're Cascadia now and you have my protection and status."

He tried to focus on her words because the intensity of what he felt for the woman in his arms nearly felled him. How he could have ever compared his feelings for Nina to a mate bond was beyond him. While he'd protect Nina and for that matter, Lex or anyone else in his family, with his life, Grace *was* his life.

He wanted to wrap her in cotton and put her on top of the

highest mountain to keep her safe. He wanted to take her out into the streets and shout out loud that she was his. Pride, protectiveness, desire, satisfaction, love, above all, love, pulsed through their bond link.

"I had no idea," he said into her hair as he breathed her scent, taking it into himself.

She turned to straddle his lap so she could look into his face. "About what?"

He groaned as she kissed along his jaw.

"I thought I had an idea of what it was to be mated. I thought the anchor bond was enough like a mate bond that I understood. But this is nothing like that. Or rather, that is nothing like this. I'm glad I didn't know or waiting for you would have been torture."

He yelped when she bit him.

"Hey! What was that for?"

"That," she said, those amber eyes sparking at him, "is for bringing up your anchor *twice* with me naked beside you. Is the baby she's carrying yours?"

Her jealousy slid through their link. Shy yes, unassuming? Nope.

"No. Grace, honey, I anchored her over two years ago now. It was just the once. She's my brother's wife, I'd never betray him, or my bond to her that way. Or you, Grace, or you."

She snorted and he held onto his wariness.

"She adores Lex. Period. I adore you. Period. There's no issue here, honey. She'll be very happy for me, and for you. You'll like her."

She scrambled off his lap and the sun streaming through the window blinds caressed her pale skin.

"You're so beautiful. I want you again and again."

She rolled her eyes but smiled and he relaxed a bit.

"I want nothing more than that. But we should be getting back. I haven't explained why the virus did what it did to the Great Lakes Enforcer."

She pulled on her clothes as he watched, loving the economic way she moved as she brushed her hair, smoothing it back into place from the sex-tousled mess it'd been just moments before.

He'd have to inform everyone back home and ready things for her there. She'd need a full-time guard as well.

"What are you thinking about?" she asked as he helped her into the car.

"Making you safe. Making you at home in our house. Fucking you again. Your mouth wrapped around my cock. The sounds you made when I slid into you from behind."

He pinched his bottom lip. "Damn, shouldn't have said all that, now I'm hard again."

She laughed. "Good."

Everyone was still at the house when they got back. Lunch had been ordered and Cade realized how very hungry he was all the sudden.

"Can I get some of that for me and Grace, please?" he asked, indicating the platters on the sideboard.

"I'll get it." Grace moved but Megan put a hand on her arm with a smile.

"Welcome to the family, Grace. I'm so glad to have you with us." Megan hugged Grace, who after a moment of hesitant surprise, hugged her back.

"Thank you."

His woman blushed. Cade liked that a lot.

"Sit down, Grace. You're an Alpha now. Let us help." Megan indicated a chair next to Cade.

"Don't be silly. I may be an Alpha but I'm not an invalid. And you're not my servant. That's not how I am, you should know that now, Cade Warden." She turned and gave him a look. He laughed and put his hands up.

"I'm sure you aren't, honey. I cook ninety percent of the time at home, I swear."

"Nina makes fun of all the cookies he bakes when he's stressed," Tegan laughed as Grace filled plates for the two of them.

He saw, and felt, Grace stiffen at Nina's name. Shit, this was going to be an issue.

Tee noticed too and shifted her eyes to Cade briefly and he shook his head once.

"Don't go talking behind my back, Cade. If you have nothing to hide, say it to my face." Grace practically tossed his plate on the table before sitting down with her own and tucking in.

"Later, honey. For now, let's get back to the subject at hand. The virus and you not going back to the lab here."

She glared at him momentarily before filling everyone in. "The way the virus worked was that it attacked the wolf cells in Gina's body, essentially causing her immune system to attack itself and eventually shut down. It happened very quickly, within a matter of minutes. I'm sorry. I will say, from what I understand, she gave up no information at all."

"She died with honor." Tegan took a deep breath.

"She did. A credit to her Pack. But surely you can see that not only is the virus a threat to humans, it's a weapon against wolves."

"You're coming back with me and we'll get you set up at our lab." She'd be safer there, on his land, in his territory, surrounded by his wolves. No one would have a chance to harm her.

"She definitely can't go back now that she's been claimed. She'd be in danger. She will be when Pellini finds out she's mated to you. You won't be able to keep it secret for very long," Maxwell said.

"Yes. And I don't want it to be. For now, he can wonder, but soon enough he'll know." Cade sat back, munching on a piece of bread.

"But if he doesn't know, that's power, don't you think? Once he knows I'm your mate, he'll know I'm giving you information."

"It'll make him crazy to know you're with me. It'll put him off balance. He'll wonder what you know. That'll trip him up. Anyway, I'm certainly not hiding you. You're spectacular." And if Warren Pellini came for her, Cade would kill him. The wolf had done enough damage, there would be no threat to Grace again as long as there was breath in Cade's body.

She blushed and then laughed. Her tension eased, easing his own as well.

They made some plans regarding the lab in Seattle and the next steps. National would send guards and some staff, as would Great Lakes.

After many more hours, Cade got up, stretching, knowing in a matter of minutes, he'd be back in bed with Grace.

"Cade? The anchor bond, have you taken care of it?" Tegan asked quietly.

Cade fisted his hands at his sides. Now he knew what Lex gave up two years before when they'd performed the tri-bond. To have to let another male touch her, share part of what he had, it was unthinkable. And yet, to lose this precious gift was even more untenable.

"I'd be honored," Maxwell said quietly.

"I never had to face this—" Ben moved close, "—thank God. But if I had, I'm not sure I'd want to come in contact with that other guy very often. You'll be here often enough to visit us."

Cade did know. He saw Nina every day of his life. Had often yearned for more than he could ever have with her. Now, that was not gone so much as muted. Grace was everything and what he felt for Nina was love surely, but not desire. But Maxwell wasn't mated.

"I think Ben is right. I'm high level, Cade and I live across the country. You'd have very little call to see me. I'd be honored to be your anchor." Jack stood forward.

"I hate this whole thing," Megan said in an undertone. "Like she's meat. Will this be what it's like for me?"

"Okay, Megan, I know this is hard, but don't complicate this right now. I did this once. I was there, I performed the tri-bond. It's one small moment in time and you know it's what needs to happen." Tegan hugged her sister.

Grace whacked him in the arm, getting his attention. "I'm a wolf. And I'm in the room too so don't talk around me. I was born this way. I know what needs to happen and I'm fine. But it won't be Maxwell. I can't." She turned to Maxwell, who cringed. "I understand you did what you had to do in a difficult situation but I don't want to be tied to you like that." Maxwell nodded and sighed.

"I am sorry. I see it was a bad decision on my part. Hasty because I'd reached the end of my rope and wanted to protect the rest of the Pack. But it was wrong. I wronged you and I apologize. I hope you can get past that." Maxwell hung his head, giving her the respect the situation called for and Cade respected the other male for it.

Grace nodded. “Thank you, Maxwell. Cade, can we just, I don’t know, make a decision? It’s been a long, very trying day. Week. Months.” Grace took Cade’s hand and kissed it. “The tri-bond can wait until tomorrow.”

“You’re right, honey.” He hugged her to his side before turning to Jack. “We’d be honored for you to be our anchor. But Grace is right, it’s been a long day, can this wait until tomorrow?”

Jack nodded. “Of course. I’m not leaving for Boston until the mid afternoon. Shall I come by at eleven or so?”

Cade looked to Grace, who nodded. “Thank you, Jack.”

Jack laughed. “Well, um, at the risk of Cade going feral on my ass, it’s not like it’ll be a chore.”

Grace ducked her head, hiding a smile.

“Please let me extend the cottage to you until you’re ready to go back home,” Maxwell said.

“I’ll put guards on it.” Ben spoke into his wrist mic and began to give orders and Tegan just grinned at them.

“This is the coolest. Congratulations to you both and welcome to our family, Grace. I’ll have some groceries sent over from the main house.”

“We’re going to head back tomorrow evening I think.” Cade looked to Tegan, reaching out to touch her cheek. “You’re okay? You know we support you staying here if that’s what you want, right?”

Tegan smiled. “Yeah. Thank you. I can’t wait for this insanity to end so we can live a normal life. Grace, you like to shop for shoes?”

“Um, I like to shop for books, does that count?”

Megan laughed. “You’ll fit into the family just fine. Books

are almost as good as shoes."

"All right, you two go back to the cottage. The food will be on the way right now so um, don't get busy in the kitchen unless you want company. I'll see you both tomorrow, we'll have a big luncheon after the tri-bond, send you back home in style." Tegan shoved them both to the door.

At the door to the cottage, Cade pushed her against it and kissed her senseless, holding her up against him.

She wound her arms around his neck and luxuriated in the way he felt. Each breath she took, he fed back to her, his tongue teasing in and out of her mouth. He was big and strong against her.

"Damn, I love the way you taste."

The door came open as he unlocked it while still holding her. Megan and Dave pulled up and got out.

"Um, hey there. Before you start something up there, let us get settled," Dave called to them.

Cade sighed. "Yeah. That. Welcome to the world of being an Alpha." He stepped away from her but kept an arm around her waist. "Come on in, both of you. We've got talking to do."

"You do?" Grace had only one thing on her mind and it wasn't talking.

He chuckled. "It'll be quick."

She snorted and moved to go into the house but Megan put a hand on her shoulder.

"Me first, always. Okay? A guard will always go into an unfamiliar place before you."

Grace nodded, letting Megan go into the cottage to check things out and give the signal that it was okay to follow her inside.

Dave brought up the rear and they all settled in on the couches.

"First things, set up a constant guard. I trust Ben and Tee but I want one of my own wolves out there at all times. There's a bedroom up front, you guys take that one. I want someone to go to Grace's place to pack her things. Hit it with a sweeper before you bring anything back though." Cade looked to her and she wanted to cry at how sweet he was to think of that. "Is there anything in particular you want them to bring you?"

"I'll need my paperwork. My medical license and all those papers are actually in a safe deposit box. I couldn't trust anything at my condo. He'll be watching, you know."

"We know. But we'll be careful. Dave will go in and we'll set up with some of Ben's wolves to keep watch. When will they start looking for you?" Megan asked.

"Tomorrow morning most likely. I had today off. He seems to watch me less these days but I think he's got something in my car to track it. I left it in my building and walked to the dentist's office before sneaking out the next building."

Megan nodded. "Smart."

"I'd like my clothes. Not what's in my closet, that's not important. But in the drawers of the dresser in my bedroom. I've got a few suitcases in my hall closet. Should I come with you, just to show you?"

Cade pulled her against him. "No. You can't go back, Grace. I'm sorry but it's too dangerous. I can't risk your safety like that."

"Okay. I understand. I have some jewelry, that's on my dresser too. A mahogany box. My laptop is in the safe deposit box." She gave them the key and address to the bank outside the city where she'd hidden her life outside the Pack before pretending to go back to her brother.

"We'll deal with the stuff in your condo tonight. Ben has agreed to take a watch here at the cottage and I'm sure Tee will too. Now you two go on and um, do what you need to do." Megan grinned. "I'll see you later."

"Dinner. I'll make us all dinner here at nine. Invite Ben and Tee too, all right?" Cade stood and everyone scattered to obey him. Grace watched the effortless way he handled being a brother and an Alpha.

When they were momentarily alone, he looked down at her with that naughty smile and tipped his head toward the bedroom they'd been in earlier. She scampered down the hall with him on her heels.

He closed the door, shutting the world outside the door and turned to her. Grace, his mate. She'd tucked her hair behind her ears and suddenly looked about ten years younger.

"How old are you?"

"Thirty-four. Why? Shouldn't we talk, you know, after?" She whipped her shirt off and the camisole followed it.

"Impatient." His heart sped at the sight of her naked breasts.

"I could hate sex. Would you prefer that?"

Startled laughter bubbled from him. "Honey, I can't help but want to fuck you every time I even think of you." He moved to her, watched her eyes widen and her hands fidget at her waist. "Do you hate sex, Grace? Because I can scent your pussy from here and that tells a different story."

"Of course not! I'm initiating it right now. You're the one prowling around and stuff. You're delaying things, Cade Warden. Do *you* hate sex?"

He smiled at her, eating her body up with his eyes. Taking

her hand in his own, he pressed her palm against the ridge of his cock threatening to burst through his pants. "You're pretty sassy when you're horny."

"Are you going to get down to it or not?" She caught her lip between her teeth and he grinned, reaching out and shoving her skirt down. "Thank God. You talk a lot."

Picking her up, he tossed her to the bed and she bounced, laughing. Quickly, he divested himself of his clothes and got on the bed over her on all fours.

"I think you like the way I talk." He licked up her torso from belly button to the hollow of her throat.

"I do," she whispered. "But I like it when you *do* things even more." She put her hands on his chest, caressing his muscles. "Then again, I like to do things too." Using her strength, she pushed him back and straddled him.

He sifted his fingers through her silky hair as she kissed down the line of his throat, and further south, growling his satisfaction when she dragged her teeth over first one nipple and then the other.

"Your body is so hard and muscled. I like that," she told him between kisses down his abdomen.

"It's hard to reply when your mouth is, oh yeah, *Christ*," he hissed when she grabbed his cock by the root and took him into her mouth. She was so freaking small against his body, the overwhelming need to protect her was simply *more* when he saw her like that. It wasn't that she was tiny, just petite. Still, so many women in his life were so big, big presences, tall, statuesque and here was his heart, just over five feet and yet, what she'd done with her brother was the bravest thing he'd known. For no other reason than because it was right.

Fate had chosen well for him, he only hoped he could be as good for her as she was for him.

Cade Warden was the most delicious banquet she'd ever tasted. One hundred percent Alpha male. Confident. Sexy. Intelligent and oh-so-powerful. Add to that ridiculously handsome with a very handy cock, a mouth that knew its business and hands just the right size to do whatever he wanted with her and Grace Pellini was one happy female.

The taste of him, the cocktail of hormones and musk, the smooth skin of his cock and the heaviness of his balls in her palm as she sucked and licked the crown and head of him—all worked to draw her into him deeper.

She wished she had more experience with oral sex. She'd only done it a handful of times, but the way he responded to her made her want to do it more, make him feel even better.

There'd be more time for this, more time to learn him with hands and mouth, more time for everything.

"Stop, Grace, honey, I'm close. I want to be inside you." His hands tightened in her hair, enough to pull her back.

"I *liked* that, Cade."

"This?" He pulled her hair, just this side of pain and shivers ran through her.

"Mmmm, that's not what I meant but that was nice too. I like having you in my mouth."

He moved her body the way he wanted her. There was something about it that made her all tingly. Any other man and she'd have slapped his hands for using his size but the way Cade did it was sexy.

"I'm afraid I'll hurt you." He situated himself between her thighs and she wrapped her calves around him.

"That's very sweet." She reached down and inched her way closer until she could guide him to her gate. "But in case you forgot, I'm a werewolf. And because we're mates and all, I'm pretty strong. Put your damned dick in me!"

A flex of his hips and he slid into her pussy. She sucked in a breath.

"You're bossy." He grinned.

"You just keep working and I'll continue. As I was saying, you're an Alpha, your mate would be one too. Meaning just because I'm short doesn't mean I'm a pushover or weak. I know I'm quiet and I've been told I'm mousey by that idiot brother of mine. But don't test me. I can kick ass and take names or however the heck you say it. I can certainly take a nice bout of healthy sex. Your doo-dad isn't so gargantuan you'd split me in half or anything." She snorted and he laughed, dipping down to kiss her.

"You know, the more I'm with you, the more I like you. Check, I'm not going to hurt you and you just said I had a small dick."

"Oh good gracious." She arched. He crouched on his knees between her thighs, probably to keep from crushing her and he was quite a bit taller so he had a point. "Are you fishing? I quite like your dick and it's very large, thankyouverymuch. Now, stop whining and do your job."

"I'd be glad to, ma'am."

She could do little more than writhe beneath him as he thrust into her body. If she'd had bigger boobs, they might have jiggled sexily or something but it didn't matter. What mattered was how good it felt to be with him. How happy he made her feel, the way he took away the fear and replaced it with something wholly wonderful.

He caught her nipples between each thumb and forefinger and shards of pleasure shattered through her.

"I love your nipples, so juicy and puffy. They're like a

conduit straight to your clit, aren't they?"

She pressed into his touch with a soft moan. If he didn't care that they were so small, why should she?

For so long she'd had no connection to anything but her job. She thought she'd never live in a Pack again, much less find her mate. The beauty of what he was to her, not just her man but the return of her full, whole life was staggering. Oh and that really nice dick.

A giggle escaped and soon she was laughing so hard she couldn't stop. Her eyes watered and Cade simply raised one eyebrow as he watched her laugh.

"I'm glad I amuse you." He leaned down to nip at her shoulder and the change in his angle brought the entire line of his cock over her clit.

Her giggle died on an intake of air as she gasped.

"Ahhh, let's see to that, shall we?"

He kept his angle, moving from her shoulder to her nipple, his tongue flicking and tracing around first one and then the other as the friction from his cock on her clit grew in intensity.

Grace grasped at his shoulders, her nails digging into his muscles as orgasm shot through her body and he continued to fuck her, hard and harder, his breath shorter and shorter.

"Damn, you feel so good," he murmured as he shoved himself deep, his fingers gripping one nipple as he spoke around the other one and came.

Cade fell to the side, and she snuggled in behind him, keeping one arm around his waist as he caught his breath. "I don't think a woman has giggled at me during sex in, well, ever."

She pressed a kiss to the small of his back. "I don't think I've giggled during sex ever before either. For the record, it was lovely. The giggles were from a funny thought. I don't think I've been relaxed or happy enough during sex or any other time really, to giggle like that before. You make me happy, Cade."

He turned and looked at her, hazel eyes taking in every line of her face. "You're a gift, Grace. It makes me sad that you've not been as happy as you deserved to be. But I promise, despite the insanity of the world right now, to spend my time giving you that happiness."

Chapter Five

As the steaks grilled, Cade handed Grace a glass of wine. Tegan settled in with Ben and Megan on the small couches in the living area. Cade liked to see how his sisters tried to make Grace comfortable and feel at ease.

He dialed home and waited as the phone rang.

"Lex Warden."

"Hey. I just wanted to call to fill you in. You with Nina right now?"

"Where the hell else would he be I ask you?"

"Hello, sweet thing. It's lovely to hear those dulcet tones," he said dryly and rolled his eyes at Megan, who snickered.

Unease trickled through his gut and he cut his eyes to Grace, who looked at him through narrowed eyes.

"What's up?" Lex interjected over the line, amusement clear in his voice.

"I met my mate today. Sealed the bond. We're coming home tomorrow night."

"You what?" Lex yelled. "Are you serious?"

"I am. She's beautiful and a doctor so you know she's smart. Her name is Grace. She's also Warren Pellini's sister and the inside source who's just handed us a huge amount of information that may end up stopping him once and for all."

Cade smiled at Grace, trying to let her know he believed in her.

"You're shitting me! You had sex with that asshole's sister? How do you know you can trust her? Cade, this is insanity." Nina's voice brought total silence to their end of the call.

Grace's eyebrows flew up and Megan put an arm around her.

"You're out of line, Nina. Grace is my mate. Of course I can trust her. She risked her life for us. For every wolf including the one in your belly."

Chaos broke out as everyone on their end started talking about the pregnancy. Grace stood up and moved to leave the room but Cade reached out to stop her, bringing her to sit in his lap.

"No. You belong here with me. She's wrong. She doesn't know you and she's worried. It'll be fine." He kissed her temple but knew she was very unhappy. His wolf, hell his human, was agitated at her dismay and troubled feelings. It was his job, the point of his life to make her happy and she most definitely wasn't right then.

"Cade, I can't believe you told everyone. I asked you to keep it quiet until after the week was up."

"Nina, I can't believe you're being this way right now with my mate here in the room," Cade shot back.

"She's jealous. Can't you hear that in her voice?" Grace said softly. "She's had you to herself all these years. And if you think other people don't feel the same way about me because of my last name you're out of your mind. It's going to be a problem. You have to know that."

"You don't know me, don't speak for me," Nina said from the other end.

"I'd ask the same of you, then. Or, are you so very special

you get to be abusive while no one else can reply?" Grace replied calmly

Well now, apparently shy had its limits with Grace. Cade smiled inwardly. Not at the strife but at her spine. The jealousy comment hit him hard. He hadn't thought of that, which had been stupid of him because of course Nina would have a hard time adjusting.

"I agree. Come on, Nina, I'm telling you, she's good people. Do you honestly think Cade would ever endanger his people by bringing in anyone who posed us harm?" Tegan said, smiling over at Grace.

"Stop trying to leave the room, Grace," he whispered in her ear. "You're the Alpha of this Pack too. Last names bedamned, you're a better wolf than most. You risked your life to get this information and no one is going to get away with attacking you in my presence."

"I'm sure we can smooth over all this trouble when you get back," Lex interjected. "Of course we're pleased you've found your mate, Cade, and I'm sure Grace is a wonderful person."

"That remains to be seen!" Nina yelled.

"I think you've got some proving to do as well, Nina. But in the long run, I don't need to prove anything to you. I'm here, get used to it." Grace pushed Cade's restraining arms away with a strength he'd only suspected and stomped out of the room muttering to herself.

"We'll be home tomorrow night. And she's right, get used to it." Cade disconnected and scrubbed his hands over his face.

"That went well." Ben chuckled. "At least no one threatened to kill her and leave her body in the woods like you did with me. All in all, a warm Warden reception."

Cade snorted. "We're not that bad. What the hell was that? Nina is a hardass yes, but I've never known her to be anything less than a compassionate, good-hearted person."

Megan just stared at him. "You're such an idiot. I love you, you're smart and strong and all the things a person should be but you have such a blind spot. Grace is right, Nina is jealous. Part of it will be hormones from the pregnancy but another part is that Nina has had you and Lex as her husbands for the last two years." She held up a hand. "Oh I know neither of you would ever overstep your boundaries and I know she's ridiculously happy with Lex and now you are with Grace. But in the time since Nina joined Cascadia, you've not dated or really had any females around. You're her anchor and let's not lie, you've been a little in love with her and she with you."

He wanted to deny it but he couldn't. Part of him had loved Nina but knew she wasn't his. Now that he'd found Grace, he understood what he'd felt was in part due to their bond and a pale shadow of what it was to really be mated.

"That's due to the bond. But what I have with Grace, well there's no comparison at all. She's my everything. Nina is my sister, my Packmate and my anchor bond but Grace is my mate. My life is about her."

"The steaks are nearly done. I'll go in and talk to her. You'll muck it all up." Tegan stood and rolled her eyes at him.

"Don't make things worse, Tee."

"Please. I've dealt with Nina long enough to know a few things. I've also dealt with you long enough to know a few things. Lastly, I have lady parts, I have a bit more to say on this score than you do. Tomorrow you will make sure everything is about her and make it clear to everyone back home." Tegan sighed and went toward the closed bedroom door where Grace had sequestered herself.

Grace scrubbed her face and moisturized before stomping

back into the bedroom. The nerve of that woman! Grace knew people thought she was either evil because of who she was or a pushover. She was neither.

You didn't have to be hard on the outside, foul mouthed, mean, snarky or bitchy to be powerful. Grace knew that. She held life and death in her hands on a daily basis. She waded into terror and blood every time she went to work. Didn't mean she had to get a God complex like some of her colleagues or affect an exterior of nonchalance so thick they didn't seem to be moved by anything.

Things moved Grace Pellini. Things got to her, touched her deeply. Made her angry and upset and insecure. That was human and she may be a werewolf but she was partly human too and unlike some others, she embraced that. *Feeling* things didn't make her weak.

Right then, she *felt* like smacking Nina Warden's bitchface. Hmpf.

She'd done her best to ignore part of the conversation out in the living room by turning on the water and washing up but she heard the steps coming down the hall toward the bedroom. Tegan, if she wasn't mistaken.

"Can I come in?" Tegan asked from the other side of the door.

"Sure." She opened the door and Tegan came into the room and sat on the bed.

Good gracious, Tegan was beautiful. So much so it made Grace uncomfortable just looking at her. She didn't usually worry about her looks and wow, she did have Cade Warden naked and willing to serve her with gusto, so it wasn't like she needed large breasts and all that gorgeous hair, but these Warden women could give a person a complex.

"I just wanted to talk with you a bit. Make sure you're okay.

The thing is, I love Nina. She's a very dear person to me. But, she's wrong here and out of line and generally just acting like a brat. You're my family now too. My sister, like she is, and I like you. I think you're incredibly brave to have done what you did and not crack. You're good for Cade, he needs something to care about other than the Pack. You're worthy of him."

"Something to care about other than the Pack and his brother's wife?"

Tegan's eyebrow went up in a very fine imitation of her oldest brother. She sighed. "Astute. But I'm not sure it's that simple. And certainly not accurate at this point anyway. He loves you. I've been mated, twice. I've had an anchor. I know what it is to feel deeply for your anchor and what it feels like to be bonded to your mate. The difference is night and day. Tomorrow you may be in a better position to understand what I'm saying after you do the tri-bond with Jack. Lex and Nina are strong together, a force of nature really. She's a very big personality. She tends to suck up the air in the room. It works because Lex needs that sort of woman to keep him in line as he can be, um, a wee bit controlling."

Tegan paused and then laughed. "Okay, a lot controlling. Now Cade lives with them in the house and he's very paternal. He's a worrier, it's his job as Alpha. I hope I don't offend you when I assume you don't know what it's like to be around an actual Alpha."

Grace shrugged. "No. Although I did grow up in a Pack, I know Warren isn't an actual Alpha. He's more like the boss of his group rather than the Alpha. There's no compulsion to obey him other than fear."

Tegan nodded. "Okay, then the thing is, Cade is no less strong than Lex. In fact, he's stronger because Lex can pour all his energy into one thing, protection. Physical protection of the

Pack. But Cade has to think about *everything.* Finances of the Pack, physical safety, boundary issues, inter-Pack relations, the relations of all the wolves in the Pack, his own family, his own position, the position of the Pack in the US and the world and now this war. He doesn't need a big presence like Nina. And I'm not saying you're not a big presence, you are. But with you, it's under the surface. You don't need to be managed. You won't hare off on a wild scheme. You're as calm and smart and far thinking as he is and that's what he needs."

"A Pellini is doubtless *not* what he needs. But he's bonded to one now and that's the breaks."

Tegan laughed. "I like you, Grace. You'll do fine. Nina is a good person, she is. She loves her husband and she loves her Pack. But you're the Alpha and Cade is yours. Stand up for it and don't let her push you around. I think the two of you will actually get along well once your roles get established. But I expect that establishing will be a bit bumpy and of course Cade just loves you and assumes that's all it takes." She stood. "And now, let's go eat. You have no idea how pouty Cade gets if the food he makes gets cold."

"I can imagine. He doesn't seem to know what it is to be disobeyed."

"Very true. He was this way even when he was a kid. If you ever need to talk, I want you to know I'm here. I mean that. The rest of my sisters are wonderful as well. Tracy is in Portland but she'll like you immediately and Layla, well, Lay is the most like Cade of all the siblings. I think you and she will really hit it off."

The two of them walked back into the small dining room area and Cade immediately came to her and enfolded her in his arms. Comfort washed through her system as she breathed him in, sinking into his body and their link.

After everyone had left, Cade pulled her body to his, already spoiled by her presence in bed with him. "I'm sorry about earlier. I didn't think. I just wanted to share the good news."

What pissed him off so much is how he rejoiced for Lex and what a fucked up response he got from them. They made his woman hurt and their reaction was selfish. He'd never actually been more hurt by Nina than earlier during that call. Even when she hated him after the fight at the Pack house that'd transformed her into a wolf he hadn't been so disappointed in her.

"Cade, you had to expect something like that. I don't like it but I'm well aware of how people react to my last name."

He turned her and she had an exasperated expression on her face. He kissed her because there was nothing else he could do when he saw the scrunched up nose. "Don't be so matter-of-fact about my brother and his wife snubbing you."

"I'm not. Believe me, Cade, I am not pleased about it and I really don't like the idea of living with them at this point. But what I do accept is that my brother has hurt so many people, the name Pellini will raise suspicion and ire."

The low burn of her anger reached through the link. He hated it. Hated that she felt bad when she should only feel joy.

"And you, stop it. You can't control everything, Cade." The link worked both ways.

"I can't help it. I was made to make you happy. I want that. It's not happening."

She nipped his shoulder and his body roared to life.

"I'm very happy. And by the feel of it, so are you."

"It's been a long day. I've taken you twice as it is." Even as he said it, he pressed his cock into her, into that fragrant, soft skin.

"Third time's a charm," she said softly, opening up to him like he was meant to be there.

And he was.

Chapter Six

"So, Jack, do you have a girlfriend? Someone who's going to be upset about this?" Grace placed a cup of coffee before Jack Meyers, the man she'd be fucking within the hour.

It wasn't that he wasn't appealing. Jack Meyers was incredibly handsome. Hot even. Surfer boy good looks, tanned, muscled, pale blue eyes and blond hair bleached by the sun. He looked as if he'd be more at home in Newport Beach rather than Boston's Back Bay.

"I had a human girlfriend but we broke up just before war was declared. As for wolves..." he shrugged, "...you know how it goes. By the time we get to my age, everyone is focused on finding their mate. Not a lot of dating, just a lot of fucking. I suspect the only person who'll be upset about this is Cade." He winked at Cade who snorted grumpily.

He'd been testy all morning long. She understood it, she was terribly unhappy that she'd have to come face to face with his anchor that very evening. But still, it wasn't like she was jonesing to have sex with a total stranger either. Even one who was as delicious as Jack was.

"Let's be honest, shall we? This is uncomfortable for both of you, I know that. But it's what we do. It's what wolves do. Our parents did, their parents did, and so on. I'm not going to lie and say I regret this. Grace, you're a beautiful wolf who's done something extraordinary. I admire that, hell I find all that courage very sexy. And I like you. I can respect a woman who'll be my anchor bond and that's the whole point, right?"

Cade nodded and reached out to squeeze Grace's hand.

"I live in Boston. You two will live in Bellevue, it's not like we'll see each other every day and when I meet my mate, I'm sure she'll be glad of it." He laughed and Grace wanted to groan. "How would you prefer we did this? Grace and me alone? All three of us? It's up to you two."

"I haven't known Grace very long or I'd just go away for half an hour but I don't like the idea of not being here, of not seeing what happens." Cade's agitation jittered through the link.

Grace stood and went to the cabinet and pulled out a bottle of Jameson's. Their metabolism would work fast to overcome the alcohol but it would take the edge off and goodness knew they all had enough edge at the moment.

She poured two stiff shots for herself and handed one to Cade and refilled it. He grinned and shrugged, taking the second and then a third.

"You don't have to drive. You want one, Jack?"

He laughed, a rich, warm sound. "I have a driver too so why not? I must say before that though, I don't need it. I'm plenty relaxed."

"Incorrigible. All male wolves when they know they're getting sex are just incorrigible," Grace muttered.

Jack laughed, drank the shots, unbuckled his belt and freed his cock.

She blinked and he sent her a grin so wicked it turned her knees to rubber.

"That's better. Enough talking, let's get to it, shall we? I was thinking, Grace, that you would look very sexy on top. So petite and lovely. But you're not ready just yet I wager so I think Cade and I need to take care of that."

"Ready?" Her brain struggled to function but the scent of aroused male wolf hung in the air, distracting her mightily. Her wolf recognized its mate in Cade and rolled against her human skin but in Jack, her wolf paused and then responded, knowing the anchor bond was there. The bond that would save a female wolf should she lose her mate. Jack would be more to her than just some other handsome male, he'd be part of her mate bond with Cade, someone very special. A male could only serve as an anchor bond if he was unmated and hadn't served as an anchor for any other female. The way the bond worked was that the higher in power a wolf was, the smaller the group of compatible anchor wolves was as well due to the need to be comparable in power or related.

"Don't think so hard, honey. Just relax and enjoy this." Cade moved to stand behind her. His lips skated up her neck briefly before he moved back long enough to pull her shirt off.

Another set of lips, this one Jack's, pressed against her belly. He undid the waist of her pants and pulled them down, along with her panties, until she stood totally naked between two Alpha wolves. She nearly giggled but held it in, letting the warmth of the alcohol slide through her system, loosening her limbs and her inhibitions.

"You're so pretty. Oh I do love breasts like yours. So perky, nipples so big and sensitive. I bet you never wear a bra." He smoothed his hands up her belly and back down her thighs, his thumbs brushing against her very wet pussy. "Lean back against Cade, sweetheart," Jack said and Cade took a step back, taking her upper body with him. Her eyes drifted closed as Cade's fingers began their tug and roll of her nipples.

She nearly jumped from her skin when Jack's tongue slid

against her clit as he pushed her thighs wide and devoured her pussy. The sensation stole her breath.

What to do with her hands? Deciding to just go for it, she sifted her fingers through Jack's hair with one hand and reached behind her to unbutton and unzip Cade's pants and grab his cock with the other. With a soft grunt in her ear, he pressed forward into her fist. He might have felt a bit tense but there wasn't much of a doubt he was pretty turned on right then.

"I like seeing his mouth on you," Cade whispered. "I like knowing he'll never be able to taste you again but I know from experience that your taste is unforgettable."

How did he do that? Her body shivered in response as Jack's tongue lapped at her pussy. Orgasm approached quickly and stole over her as she arched back into Cade.

He lifted her up and over Jack and she found herself sliding down his cock.

"Sweet Christ. Grace, you're so tight," Jack gasped out.

"It's a good thing the alcohol hasn't affected your staying power," she moaned and Cade bit the back of her neck.

"What the hell did you just do? Her cunt rippled around me and nearly made me come right then."

"I know my woman. Know her taste. Know the feel of the delicate skin just at the back of her neck." He said it like a taunt and Jack laughed.

"But my cock is buried in her right now. That must suck for you. For me? Not so much."

This time Cade laughed. "Smartass."

"Hi, my name is Grace and I'm the girl in this sandwich. Can we, um, focus please? I know this is some sort of odd dominance thing you two are up to but how about you both do what needs to done to finish the tri-bond and then you can go outside and punch each other or spit or whatever you all do."

Cade answered with a tongue sliding up her spine and a series of sharp bites as he went. Jack just laughed and continued to fuck into her body with rolls of his hips. One of his hands slid between them and the other trailed down her curve of her ass. Suddenly fingers worked in concert, some on her clit, the others tickling across her ass and against her perineum.

A strangled gasp of pleasure came from her and she started to lean forward against Jack's chest but Cade brought her against him, his mouth moving to hers, swallowing the sounds she made, even as climax came. His eyes held hers, not giving her the room to think about anything but him.

"Enjoy it, honey, but don't forget who'll be delivering your pleasure every day until the end of time," he said against her lips.

Never had she been with anyone who was so dominant, so powerful and totally sure of his allure. It was overwhelming and as much as it sort of embarrassed her to admit, totally and ridiculously sexy.

"Bastard," Jack grunted and came, holding her hard against him tight.

Cade laughed, his hair tickled her cheek. "You got that right."

Jack gave a long, satisfied sigh and the anchor bond began to settle and take root, knocking her off balance. Cade picked her up and held her against his body, rocking back and forth, speaking softly. Jack slowly stroked up and down her leg and after a bit, she began to calm and come back to herself.

"Thank you, Jack. Truly." Cade shook Jack's hand. Jack took the hint and after pressing a kiss to Grace's still bare shoulder, stood and tucked himself back in his pants.

"It's an honor. Grace, sweetheart, thank you for sharing yourself with me. Should you ever need anything you know to come to me, right?"

Grace looked up at him through her hair and blushed, staying pressed against Cade to hide her nakedness. Cade liked that.

"Cade, I'll be speaking to you soon. Keep us apprised of the situation with the virus, all right? Grace, you take care of yourself and don't let anyone push you around. You're a brave woman and my anchor. Be well and keep Cade in line."

"Thank you, Jack. Please be safe." Grace sat up but Cade put his arm around her, over her breasts and she leaned into him.

"You too, sweetheart. I only hope my mate is half as special as you are."

And with that, he grabbed his bag, slipped on his shoes and was gone, leaving them there alone.

She was safe and their bond was complete. For a moment Cade let himself be totally satisfied.

"How about a bath? I'll wash your hair and get to all those hard to reach spots." He kissed the top of her hair.

"Extra hot?"

"Small price to pay to see you naked and wet, I must say." Standing, he continued to hold her as he made his way toward the bathroom. He liked how small she felt against him, as sexist as it probably was, he had to admit he dug their size difference. Especially because he knew it didn't have a darned thing to do with her strength.

Chapter Seven

"It's going to be just fine," Dave said as he moved in front of Grace. Dave had become Cade's full-time guard when Lex had met Nina and Megan was Nina's guard. Not wanting to complicate matters any further by raising resentment against Grace if he took Megan from Nina, Cade ordered Megan, who was now the head of Lex's Enforcers, to appoint a guard for Grace immediately upon their return.

Cade didn't know if it would be just fine or not, but he appreciated his cousin's sentiment nonetheless. Dave had taken to Grace right away. The two were a lot alike, Dave very rarely said anything unless he had to either. Dave could snap a neck with lightning speed of course, and he topped nearly seven feet tall, making Grace look even tinier, but still.

"What are you snorting about?" Grace asked as he grabbed her hand and kissed it. They were making their way off the plane and toward the satellite room where he could see a whole mess of Wardens gathered.

"Nothing. Have I told you how beautiful you look?"

"Only fourteen times. But fifteen won't hurt. Look, I'm not going to run away. This won't be easy of course, but you're mine and I didn't make it through med school and get through every day in an emergency room without breaking by being a pushover."

Her hair was pulled back and a delicate strand of freshwater pearls lay against the pale skin of her neck. Her sweater was cashmere, the slacks a soft wool. She looked elegant and regal. She looked like a queen.

He saw his parents. His mother wore a big smile and pushed away from the group to approach with her hands open to take Grace's.

"Grace, honey, this is my mother, Beth Warden."

"I'm so pleased to meet you, Grace. Welcome to our family and to our Pack. We've waited a long time for you."

Well that was easier than he thought. His mother's support would go a long way toward how any of the other wolves would feel about Grace.

"Welcome to Cascadia. I'm Henri, Cade's father. Be at home in our family." He bent and kissed each one of Grace's cheeks after giving the official words to welcome her to the Pack.

Lex walked forward. "Nina is still in bed. She insisted I come." He gave Grace a once over and Grace raised one of her eyebrows and gave him one right back, her arms crossed over her chest.

The group remained silent until Layla pushed forward. "Get over it, Lex," she muttered before looking to Grace. "My goodness, you're lovely. I'm Layla and we're so glad to have you. We have better manners than this. I apologize." She jerked her head toward Lex.

Grace stepped forward and took Layla's hands. "Thank you." She looked to his parents. "And thank you. Your welcome means a lot to me. I didn't have any real family life since the Pellinis were shunned from Great Lakes. I left my family and lived outside the world of wolves."

"Let's get out of the open, please." Dave put a hand at the small of Grace's back and urged them all forward.

"Yes, let's go home. Nina will be anxious."

"How's she been?" Cade asked his brother quietly. Grace tensed up and pulled away from him and he gritted his teeth a moment.

"Worried."

At the cars, Grace had positioned herself next to Dave with his father on her other side. "Why don't you ride with Lex?" she asked blandly before turning back to his father who got the pretty smile he should have received.

Megan smacked his arm and shoved him in the other car. "You're both total fucking idiots," she growled as she pulled away, following the other cars back to the house.

"What?"

"You, Lex, I should kick you in the junk for not even welcoming *your Alpha* to the Pack. Your brother's mate. Asshole! And you, Cade, what is your problem? You didn't even introduce her to Lex. No, you asked about Nina."

She took a corner sharply and he had to hold on.

Lex swore colorfully. "I had her checked out. She's clean. She's been working at the public hospital for four years in the emergency room. She graduated at the top of her class. She could be making a hell of a lot more in private practice, by the way. She took a leave of absence seven months ago. No arrest record. Lots of public service. Started a program getting medical services out on the streets to the homeless population."

"You did a background check on my mate?" Outrage at his brother coursed through Cade.

"I did a background check on *my* mate too. It's what I do, Cade. Your judgment is clouded by the mate bond. Mine isn't."

"Is that so? You don't even know her and you've judged her. She can't help who her brother is but damn it if she didn't risk her life to get us the information she did. She saw someone hurting in her ER and she gave up her entire life to help. That says more than any background check you could have." Cade had wanted to pop his brother in the nose more than a few times in his life but never more than that moment.

"You're bringing her home to live in the same house as my wife and child. I won't apologize for checking her out. The Pack is my responsibility too. I had to be sure you weren't thinking with your dick."

Megan hit the brakes a bit hard then and Cade saw the flash in her eyes in the rearview.

"Fuck. You. If you don't like it, move your ass out. I won't have my wife, my mate, treated with anything less than the respect she's due. She's your Alpha, Lex."

"I know."

"What?"

"She's on the level. She's my Alpha and she's due my respect."

Cade turned and glared at his brother. "You got me in trouble with her over this?"

"HA!" Megan exploded from the front seat. "You got yourself in trouble asking about Nina right after Lex snubbed her. She might be little but the both of you better wear a cup for a while."

"I didn't snub her. I just wanted to get a feel for what she was like. She's strong. A tiny little thing for Christ's sake, but tough. I suppose you don't deal with the hell of an ER for years without being hard. She just sounds so soft and gentle." Lex chuckled. "She and Nina are going to clash."

"I know. But Lex, my responsibility is Grace. So Nina has to deal. Her week is nearly up. I can't keep Grace from living fully in her own house."

"Her week is up tomorrow and she's already chomping at the bit to get up and move around. The doctor was over this morning and everything seems fine with the baby. I suggest we back off and let the two of them find their way through this. Nina loves you and she only wants the best for you and the Pack. Pellini had her brother killed."

"*Warren* Pellini did. Grace had nothing to do with that. And Nina has a fucking criminal record, I didn't flip out about that. What has Grace done except have the bad luck of who she was born with?"

The cars began to pull up the long drive to the house. Two more checkpoints had been added since the declaration of war so it took longer than normal and by the time Megan got the car pulled into the garage, Grace was already on her way inside with her bags being carried by one of the other wolves.

"I've decided to assign Evan to you, Cade and Dave will work with Grace. It'll be best that way. He knows her and likes her. She'll be more comfortable I think. *Someone* needs to think of her comfort," Megan snapped before she got out and scanned the area while Lex and Cade went into the house, following the noise.

The nerve of the man. Grace sat as far away from Cade as she possibly could, right between his mother and grandmother. She wasn't going to run in and check on Nina, that was for sure.

Lex disappeared and Grace could tell Cade wanted to follow but instead approached her. She turned to listen to his grandmother but Cade just knelt at her feet and took her hands in his.

"Honey, would you like a tour of our house? See the deck in

the moonlight? Let me apologize?"

She withheld an undignified snort but his grandmother laughed. "Very nicely done, Cade. Your grandfather would have been proud. Saw him on his knees like that to me more than once. I suggest jewelry to go with it next time. And there will be a next time, Grace. That's who the Warden men are."

Beth put her arm around Grace and squeezed. "Things won't be easy for a bit. I know people will judge you for your name. But your name is Warden now and they'll have me to contend with. Go on, forgive him and then go meet Nina. She's having a bit of a sulk I imagine. I'll go in when you two go on the tour. I'm sure you've heard this but I'll say it too, Nina is a good person. She's protective and she loves this Pack. She's had Cade to herself for a long time and she won't want to share at first but she'll realize she has to. Because Cade is yours as surely as Lex is hers. Now that you've got an anchor perhaps you might understand that a bit more. I don't make excuses for rudeness, believe me some people named Lex and Nina are going to hear from me on that score. But I do believe in second chances and I hope you do too." She kissed Grace's temple and waited for Grace to look at Cade, sigh and hold out her hand to let him help her up.

Grace did understand a bit. She felt a connection to Jack, even with the distance. He felt *hers* in some sense and if they all lived under one roof it would have been more difficult. But still, Cade was hers, even if he was being an ass.

He tucked her hand in the crook of his arm and led her through to the kitchen. A woman's touch was evident in the large space. Not a decorating choice she'd have made, but it wasn't bad.

"The kitchen." He opened French doors and they went out onto a huge deck that wrapped around the entire back of the house.

She moved to the railing and looked out over the trees and the city beyond in the distance.

"Beautiful isn't it? This is all Cascadia land. Safe to run on at any time. We've stepped up security of course but just let Dave know and feel free. I'd like to run with you but if I'm not around." He shrugged. "I'm sorry. I really am. I didn't mean to make you feel bad. I ripped Lex a new one in the car on the way back. He realizes he misjudged you and I expect he'll say the same to you himself. I love you, Grace. I want you to be happy."

She sighed. He was an Alpha, a worrier and he clearly cared about his family. They'd only been together a few days so she could get past a few missteps until they got used to each other.

"I love you too, Cade. And I forgive you."

He kissed her softly as the sound of the trees in the wind wrapped around the noise from inside. The beating of hearts soothed her jangled nerves.

"Let's see the rest."

He took her back inside, showed her the security offices where Lex's Enforcers worked and back up to his office. Around a corner and large double doors stood open and she saw her bags.

"This is our room. I'm sure you'll want to change the décor. It's been this way since the house was finished ten years ago. On the opposite side of the house from Lex and Nina, by the way. Bulletproof glass on the windows and there are special sensors on the deck. Motion lights, all that jazz. So we get the quiet but it's locked up tight over here too. I'm giving you one of the Mercedes to drive, by the way. At first though, I'd ask that you be escorted everywhere. We'll get you to the lab within the next few days. But I want you to myself for a bit."

"The lab?"

"I assumed you'd want to be there. If I'm wrong, well, you can do anything you'd like. Stay home, work. Whatever."

Grace leaned into his chest, loving the way his arms automatically slipped around her. "No. I want to work in the lab. I just didn't want to make any assumptions."

"You're obviously qualified, Grace. You did the work with Warren's virus samples, you're the logical choice. I spoke with our lead researcher briefly this morning and he's quite interested in meeting you. We sent the data ahead and he says you took a lot of risks." He frowned down at her as she looked up into his face.

She shrugged. "I did what needed to be done. I wish it had been more but he had so much security when I finally got access it was hard. I shouldn't have left so early."

"Stop that right now. I wouldn't have met you if you'd waited. You're mine, fate brought you to me, Grace. You're where you need to be. Do you want to rest or go back out?"

"Let's go and meet Nina." She sighed. The woman needed to know a few things. First that Grace was her Alpha. Second and more importantly, Cade was *hers* and the time for two sort-of husbands was over. And hell, everyone seemed to really like Nina so she'd have to give the woman a fair shake.

"You sure?"

"Yes."

He smiled and kept his arm around her as he guided her back across the house to where Lex and Nina's room was.

Nina's face split into a grin when she saw Cade but she frowned when she caught sight of the tiny, classy, beautiful woman at his side. He had his arm around her like she was a precious and fragile thing. Their bond emanated from them and it hit her square in the gut.

Lex had explained to her that the background check was clean and that Grace Pellini had done a brave thing and risked her life to help them. Nina had to give the woman props, what she'd done scared the hell out of her just hearing it and after knowing what Warren Pellini's thugs had done to the Enforcer of Great Lakes, it was even more frightening.

Still, Nina felt territorial. This was her house and she'd known and loved Cade longer.

Lex stood and lowered his head to them. "Grace, I wanted to apologize to you for my behavior earlier. It was rude and beneath me and you deserved better. Welcome to Cascadia and to our family."

Grace touched the back of Lex's neck and Nina actually growled. She hadn't meant to, she'd just wanted to think a growl at that miniature Audrey Hepburn and her freaking regal-looking clothing and those damned pearls.

Instead, Cade's gaze shot up and met hers and Grace finished touching Lex's neck before standing back and stepping around him to look Nina square in the face.

Well, she might be no bigger than a Hershey's kiss, but Tiny there was a fucking Alpha through and through. Amber-colored eyes took Nina in from head to toe, cool and assessing.

"You must be Nina. Did you have something to add?"

If she thought she was getting an apology, she was out of her mind. "No."

"I'd hoped to be surprised. I suppose I'm too old to be surprised anymore." She turned to Lex and nodded. "Apology accepted. If you'll excuse me, I think I'll go make some tea." Those eyes landed on Nina again. "I could say it was a pleasure to meet you, or something similar but equally false. But we both know that'd be a lie. Instead, let me say, I'm here to stay. You get your rest, the baby needs it."

She turned on her expensive little heels and left the room, head held high and Nina sort of liked the little bitch.

Cade shook his head. "Nina..."

"Don't you Nina me, Cade Warden. I was here first. I won't apologize for watching over my dudes."

"I'm not your dude. Grace is right, rest up. I'll see you in the morning." He turned and left and Lex looked at her with a sigh.

"Beautiful, you know I can refuse you nothing. You know I adore you and the baby you carry. But you can't go on like this. It's not good for you or the baby. And she's not half bad you know. He's not yours."

She saw the hurt flash in his eyes and reached up to touch his face. "Alexander Warden, I love you. *You.* You know of course, Cade and I are fond of each other and the tri-bond was very close for us. But the way I feel about you has never, ever been in doubt. I'm getting stretch marks just for you. I even let you tell your mother tonight about the baby, didn't I? She'll never leave me alone now." Her mother-in-law had the worst case of grandbaby lust of anyone she'd ever known. She had grandchildren already, two of them, and still it wasn't enough. Beth was greedy.

"You have to let go of him, Nina. She's good for him. It's the way of things. Having him with us without a mate meant he led a whisper of a life while you and I had a full one. That's not love. That's selfish."

She smiled. Her dude was wicked smart for such a big tool. "I hate when you're smarter than me. Does she have to be so fucking pretty and classy? All, *I'm a doctor and I wear pearls* and shit? And what, is she like one of those miniature dolls the rich girls kept in glass cases? She's teeny! What's up with that?"

He snorted but the beginning of his smile returned. "You're looking for things to not like about her."

"She's a Pellini, Lex. That's enough. They killed my brother."

"She didn't have anything to do with that. No more than you had anything to do with Rey when he broke the law. I adore you and I know you want what's best for this Pack. You're going to have to get along with her. Hell, I'd wager you'll even like her. If you give her a chance."

"Hmpf. Maybe."

Cade caught up with her in their room as she tossed a suitcase on the bed and unzipped it.

"I realize you're worried about your sister-in-law. I'm a doctor, I know how risky it is for humans turned wolf in the first week. But I don't share, Cade. Period. I won't live that way. If that's what she expects, that expectation needs to be eradicated. If that's what you expected, you need to say so right now so I can leave." The eyes that greeted his sparked with fury.

She might look sweet but she got right down to the point. In truth the way she'd acted with Nina flipped his switch in a major way. She truly was his mate, truly was an Alpha.

"Grace, honey, I'd kill any wolf who suggested sharing. I don't share either. Jack got his taste but that's it forever. You're mine. I'm yours. You're not going anywhere. And hell, neither is she. You handled her just fine. She'll respect your strength and when she thinks about it, she'll realize she's being silly and stop being a bitch."

"She'd better, Cade." She paused, staying there with the

bed between them. "Do you love her?"

He felt her uncertainty, her pain and could do nothing else but go to her and fall to his knees. "I love her, yes. She's my anchor bond and my sister-in-law. More than that, she's my friend. She's been with me through a lot of stuff. She's the other half of my brother. Lex and I may be at odds every now and again but he's my best friend." He put his arms around Grace's waist and breathed her in.

Her body remained stiff as she processed what he'd said.

"But that wasn't your question, was it? Do I love her romantically? Sexually? Like I love you?" He looked up into her face and she touched the side of his jaw, softly, gently. "No. At one time, I think I did. Or I thought I knew what it was to love. Partly it was the link, I'm sure Jack feels deeply for you and over time that would grow. Partly it's because Lex and I are brothers. Our feelings for each others' mates would be complicated by our biological link to each other. What I feel for you, Grace, *nothing* in the universe could have prepared me for. There's no issue of choice, of choosing between you and anyone else. I've chosen. I chose the moment I saw you the first time. I don't want you to hurt, Grace. If the idea that I would take my eyes from you for a single moment bothers you, rest assured, that's not the case."

She got to her knees, facing him and kissed along the line of his jaw. "Good. Now I won't have to maim you in your sleep and start a whole new level of Clan war. I love you too, or I wouldn't stay here and deal with this business." She stood and held out her hand. "Now, come on, we have a house full of people to entertain."

"I'm so going to nail you when everyone leaves." He looked her over with a wicked grin.

"I'm counting on it."

Chapter Eight

Grace bustled around the kitchen the next morning, her muscles sore in all the right places. She reached up to brush her fingertips over the spot on her neck where Cade had bitten and marked her as he took her from behind only an hour before.

He'd woken her up, hunger on his face and they'd made love with silent intensity as the sun came up and warmed the room and their bare skin. The man was quite inventive in bed. Which was nice given her vanilla past. The sex she'd had before had been all right but fairly uninspired. Sex with Cade was full of wonderful surprises and it was just a few days.

"Well now, that's an interesting look on your face." Lex strolled into the kitchen.

"Good morning. Your brother makes me smile, what can I say? I'm making breakfast, are you hungry? Has Nina eaten yet?" She bustled around, stirring the eggs, turning the bacon, checking on the biscuits in the oven.

"You make it pretty impossible not to like you."

She turned and looked at him. He grinned back, looking a lot like Cade at that moment and she shook her head. "I'm not the enemy, you know."

"I do know that. I'm truly sorry for being so suspicious and not being warmer toward you. And if you wanted to share your breakfast with me and Nina, I'd appreciate it. I was just coming down before she woke up. Today is the all clear day so she'll be pushing me to let her up."

She turned back to the stove and pulled the eggs off the flame before spooning them into a large bowl. "You can put this on the table if you like. I've got shredded cheese, diced tomatoes and some salsa and green onions there too. Plates are out. Coffee is made although hold off for Nina until she's checked out. The caffeine can agitate blood pressure in former humans."

In another few moves, she'd pulled out the biscuits and covered them with a towel and had finished with the bacon and hash browns. Wolves did love a big breakfast and she was usually in too great a hurry to treat herself to one at home.

"Grace? Honey, your cell phone is ringing," Cade called out as he came downstairs toward the kitchen.

"I'm down here," she replied, moving to meet him at the bottom of the stairs. He kissed her quickly and handed her the phone.

"Hello?"

"Is it true?" Warren screamed into the phone. She held it away from her ear.

"Is what true, Warren?" She'd known this moment would occur, in fact, had wondered why it'd taken so long. At the same time, she was glad there were several states between them just then.

Cade and Lex both moved to her, each man touching her to calm her.

"You betrayed me! You bitch, I'll kill you for this." Warren snarled, his oily veneer stripped away. She'd seen him like this a few times before, once when he'd nearly beaten her to death when she was a teenager.

"For what, Warren?" Why she was deliberately baiting him she didn't know. Maybe he'd have a stroke and die, saving everyone the trouble of a war.

"You've mated with Cade Warden, you've given him information about my labs. Don't think I didn't know."

"Well, as it happens, I'd made an appointment to give the National Pack Aligned wolves the information about your little secret torture program and when I walked into the room Cade was there and he turned out to be my mate. I didn't plan that part, only the part where I exposed your sick and disgusting predilection for bringing pain to others." Her voice remained utterly calm. "And now here I am, Alpha of Cascadia. Golly, funny how that works, isn't it?"

Lex snorted a laugh and Cade just shook his head and held his hand out for the phone. She shrugged and handed it to him. As far as Grace was concerned, she was done playing games with Warren so let Cade take over if he chose.

"Why hello, Warren. Or, should I say, brother? You've been a very naughty boy. Imagine putting sweet Grace in a position of having to come to us with your data. And what data it is. My, if you weren't marked for death before that for daring to hurt my sister and bringing so much misery to the world because you weren't born an Alpha for real, like me, you'd have earned it with this information. Now. We've established a few things. First, Grace is my mate and my wife and she's now Alpha of Cascadia. That means she's mine to protect and has the position and power of this Pack behind her. It would be *very* silly of you to attempt to harm her. Just sayin'. We've also learned you're outmatched and if you were smart, you'd give it up and get out of Dodge. Sadly, every single experience I've ever had with you proves that you're a little boy dressing up in his daddy's clothes. They don't fit, Warren. You're not an Alpha. You're just a sad little boy, twisted and marked for death. Don't call my wife again."

He disconnected and handed Grace the phone.

"Well, breakfast will be cold. Come on." She patted Lex's arm and leaned in to kiss Cade and walked past them both into the kitchen.

"Lex, you sit. I'm going to take this in to Nina."

Lex started to speak but she shook her head. "No. It needs to be done. I'm a doctor and I'm the Alpha here and this silliness needs to be overcome if we're all to live here in the same house. It'll be better if you let me do this on my own."

Grace made up two plates, heaped them both with food. Poured two glasses of juice and another of milk and put them on a tray and headed up to deal with Nina once and for all.

When she toed the door open Nina sat on the bed, a book in her hands. "About time." She looked up and frowned. "Oh."

"Yes, yes, you were expecting Lex but you got me. Good thing I'm a doctor who's dealt with pregnant wolves enough to know if you can get out of bed. Not that I'd let you without your own doctor's okay. I don't want to step on any toes." She put her own plate down and handed Nina the tray. "Eat."

"I'm sure the Pack doctor will be here soon. You don't need to stay. I'll wait for her."

"Oh shut up. God, you're a pain in the ass. What's your deal anyway? You're gorgeous, you have a great man like Lex, the Wardens love you. And yet, you have some unreasonable thing about me. Well, too damned bad. I said eat. Or are you going to be so stupid about this you withhold nutrition from the baby?"

Nina narrowed her eyes but began to eat anyway. "Cade's a good cook." Nina smirked and Grace laughed.

"Yes, he is. But in this case, I made breakfast." She dabbed her mouth with her napkin and settled in. "Look, here's the deal. Cade Warden is a strong, sexy, smart wolf. He's also mine. Not yours. Never was yours. He's your brother-in-law and your anchor. I hope you enjoyed having sex with him because it'll never happen again and we both know it. More importantly, *he* knows it." Grace held up her hand to keep Bitchface silent. "Oh please, don't waste my time with denials."

"You think I'm gorgeous?"

"Needy too apparently. Anyone with eyes can see it. All that hair and the skin and the boobs. God."

"So you keep the bitch all stored up so you can spring in on people at your whim?"

Grace liked Nina despite herself. Still. "Better than just spewing it all over the place at random. Did you get an extra helping of boobs at the expense of your common sense or what?"

Nina actually laughed out loud. "You'll make me choke on these rubbery eggs."

"Rubbery? I thought they were good? And you'd better hope your precious Pack doctor knows the Heimlich. I wouldn't want to waste it."

"Oh good one." Nina continued to laugh. "Fuck. I think I may actually like you. Damn you and your teeny little hide."

"That's good, I thought I might have to kick your ass and that would make Cade unhappy. I hear he bakes cookies when he's unhappy though. Hmm. Too bad you're all with child and stuff."

"Oh dear, I think, yeah, I think we may end up being BFF. Oh what is the world coming to? They're good cookies though. Damn, I really wanted to hate you. You and your cute little Audrey Hepburn thing. What's up with that? Do you practice being all dignified and stuff?"

"Like in front of the mirror? No, it comes naturally. Some of us simply have it. And others..." Grace paused and sighed, looking at the other woman, "...don't. Now eat your eggs or I'll order daily enemas."

"They're cold now, but I suppose I'll power though. Do you think we should tell the two wolves listening at the bottom of the stairs to come in?"

Grace laughed. "I think they might have been hoping for a pillow fight or something."

Startled male laughter echoed up the stairs.

"We can get into a lot of trouble together." Nina winked. "You two may as well come in, we know you're there," she called out.

First Lex and then Cade came into the room, both looking wary.

"Everything okay in here?" Cade tried to hide the beginnings of a smile on his face.

"Quit it. We know you heard everything. Teeny McAlpha here got all rough with me and threatened to make me wear pearls if I don't keep in line. I took one for the team and ate her rubbery eggs. I hope you'll take note of how magnanimous I'm being."

"Must be why you ate four biscuits." Grace's eyebrow slid up.

"Must be. So okay, no more chick tension or anything. Détente has been achieved. Now where's the doctor? I have stuff to do." Nina tried to reach the phone and Lex took it away.

"You've already called her once. She said she'd be over when she could get here this morning." Lex kissed the top of her head and Cade put his arm around Grace. It felt remarkably normal and for a moment, Grace forgot they were at war and her brother was attempting to develop a biological weapon for use against his own people.

"Can you make with the doctor thing and give me the thumbs up? I've been in this bed for a week now and I just want to go for a run, shop for shoes, something other than sit in this bed." Nina looked to Grace.

"If you like I can speak with the other doctor and take over your care but I don't want to interfere until I talk to her. I don't know your history and what she's got planned for you so it's not a good idea. If she hasn't come by in an hour I'll try and contact her." Despite herself, Grace liked the idea that Nina trusted her enough to ask.

"You sure you two don't want to, you know, pillow fight? Just a little?" Lex grinned wolfishly and Cade burst out laughing.

Grace shook her head.

"I think I'm going to see how Dave is doing. I want to take a run. Nina, behave and stay in bed. It's just a little while to go and then you'll have the all clear."

"I'll come with you. It's been a week since I've gone on one. And yes, Lex, I'll take an escort along with us."

Without looking back, Cade escorted her from the room, his eyes on hers.

"You're a whole bundle of surprises, Grace. You handled that really well." Cade didn't want to go on a run, he wanted to fuck her.

"I notice you're moving me toward our bedroom, Cade."

She didn't resist though, instead leaning into him as they walked.

"We can go for a run afterward. If you can still walk." He

moved them through the door, slamming it behind himself. "I'm going to have to share you in the next day or two. With the lab and with the rest of my family. I want to keep you in bed as long as I can. I don't think it's too much to ask."

"I'm glad you're not upset about me handling Nina and my brother."

He bumped her and she tumbled back to the mattress, her smooth composure ruffled as her hair tousled and the hem of her shirt slid up, exposing a slice of smooth, pale belly.

"More than not upset, turned on. Honey, I'm an Alpha wolf, I like it when you're hardcore, especially because you're so normally calm and sweet. When you show your claws, it makes me want to put you on the nearest flat surface and shove my cock into you."

She flushed, her lips parting at his words.

"Oh. When you talk that way, that's what I want too."

"I aim to please you, Grace."

One-handed, he unbuttoned and unzipped his jeans, shoving them down and kicking out of them. She got to her knees and yanked him to the bed.

"Good. What pleases me is you being still."

She straddled his body and ripped his T-shirt down the middle, kissing over his chest and belly.

"I notice I'm the only one naked here."

"I don't need to be naked to do this." She traced her tongue, wet and warm, down the line of his cock and back up again.

What he loved so much about her was the way she openly approached everything. It was clear she wasn't an old hand at oral sex but she obviously loved doing it. Loved making him feel good and sexy and damn if that wasn't hotter than the sun.

She learned him with her hands and mouth. Tried new

things, repeating them when he responded positively. When she dipped her head to trace his balls with the tip of her tongue, he nearly jumped from his skin, especially when she gave a growl. She hadn't done that yet during sex. He liked it, it was soft and feminine like she was. Sexy.

"Honey, I'm very close, come on up here."

She moved her gaze to his and took him into her mouth as deeply as she could, to underline her point. Okay, she wasn't going to stop until he came, which was fine. He had a good recovery time and there were other things he could do in the meantime.

Never letting him go with her eyes, she continued to slowly take him in and out of her mouth, her hands working the root of him and cupping his balls. Her sweet little ass swayed in the air as she sucked him. Total perfection.

Suddenly, she sucked harder than she'd been doing and it caught him by surprise. Wave after wave of pleasure rocked him as he came, his fingers digging into the blankets, groaning out her name.

His vision was still partially blurry as he watched her touch a finger to the corner of her mouth and her tongue followed. He nearly came again at the sexy, and yet totally unconscious motion.

"You're going to kill me with the sexy. Come here, honey."

She slid up his body and came to rest, laying on top of him. He kissed her, lazily, slowly, not missing any nuance of her mouth. He tasted himself and her, tasted what they made together.

He rolled her to her side and kissed down the line of her graceful neck and over the edge of her collarbone, swirling his tongue in the hollow of her throat. He feasted on the frantic beat of her heart, breathed deep of the desire that rose from her skin until it made him drunk with her.

She simply gave in and lay back, letting him touch her, caress her, kiss her. He drew his fingertips down the sleek skin of her inner arm, up to her side, following his fingers with his mouth. She squirmed beneath him with small sighs and gaspy moans.

"So beautiful, so precious and soft. I love the way you are, Grace."

She brought a gentle hand to his face, cradling his cheek as his mouth found her left nipple. It beaded against his tongue, elongating, the skin of the areola drawing tight. Barely an A cup but God above, he loved her breasts.

She arched into him and he settled between her thighs, rubbing the length of his cock through her slick pussy. Her breath caught each time the head of him brushed over her clit.

He made to continue kissing his way toward her pussy but she held onto his upper arms and shook her head.

"What? Honey, I want to lick you, taste you, make you come."

"I...oh—" her breath stuttered as he stroked over her clit again, "—that, more of that." The heat of her blush reacted to his skin and suddenly he was ready to fuck her again. But first, he had a job to finish.

"Ahh, you like this?" He rolled his hips again, this time putting a bit more pressure when his cock hit her clit.

She jumped and moaned, nodding.

"Fine with me. Your cunt is so hot and wet. I can't wait to feed my cock into your gate, filling you up. And then I'm going to come inside you, your tight body wrapped around me like I was born to be there."

She sighed, her fingers digging into his shoulders. Her legs, strong and smooth, wrapped around his thighs as she rose up when he flexed.

"That's it, take it, honey."

The growl again and her calf muscles tightened as she came, her honey hot against his cock. The scent of her drove him insane.

One arm around her waist, he spun so he sat up in bed, his back braced against the headboard and she sat over his lap. One minor adjustment and he brought her down over his cock.

A low, bass groan echoed from her lips as her head fell back, her lips slightly parted. So fucking beautiful. Unable to stop, driven by the scent of her pussy, the scent of her pleasure and her need, he leaned in and drew his teeth over her nipple, sending her writhing over his cock as he drove himself into her body again and again.

She came, pussy fluttering and clutching around him when he bit with just enough pressure to mark her. Her wolf surfaced, shining in her eyes and his responded. For long moments, he hung there on the edge of climax, staring at the other half of his mate.

Her wolf shimmered around her for a brief moment and he lost it then, lost that battle he'd been waging with his control. One last shove into her pussy and he came, holding her down on him tight as she spoke soft words against his chest where she leaned her head.

"We need to run. My wolf needs to see yours." He picked her up and walked her to the deck. He called down to Dave whose room was right below theirs that they were going on a run and stood back as she got on all fours.

The rush of power as she transformed bit at his skin like a thousand tiny shocks and suddenly she was there, small, honey-gold, staring up at him. She jerked her head and he transformed and stood next to her, sheltering her smaller body with his larger one.

A bark and he led her around the decking and out to the forest just behind the house. He scented Dave and several other wolves who'd be their guard on the run before leading Grace out into the wilds, never getting less than a few inches from her.

His wolf was moved by her, moved by the precise way she ran, by the mark her footpads left in the soft forest floor, by the grace of her muzzle and the quiet of her movements.

He wanted her all to himself, wanted to mount her, dig his teeth into her neck and bury himself inside her. Wanted to see her hanging heavy with his children. It was real to wolf and man, the immenseness of the presence of Grace in his world.

No one would threaten that.

Chapter Nine

Grace looked at the information on the screen and then back to the slide.

"What we need to do is create an anti-virus. I've got what Warren has so far. It's not a complete or whole copy of the lycanthropy virus. But you have that here. We can take elements from that and elements from what Warren has and go from there."

It was the end of the first week she'd been working in the lab and to her great relief, the rest of the staff had taken to her authority with relative ease, despite her familial ties.

"Those newest bodies in Montana are bad news. They're getting closer, I think." She sighed. "What I think we need is to focus on something to inoculate our wolves with. We've got the virus here, a perfect copy. And we've got a working copy of what Warren has. At least two versions. They're close enough in structure and I think we can work with it. I'm going to bring it up to Cade. For now—" she looked up from the slide to the wolf who was just below her in power, "—let's get a team on that. Keep two people on the data I brought with me and the samples we were couriered today from Montana, but let's get working on a vaccine."

The wolf she'd spoken to raced off to obey.

Dave cleared his throat. “Grace, it’s nine-thirty and Cade has called four times. Just five minutes ago he threatened to come here and carry you back home himself. You’ve been here since seven this morning. You’ve got to get some rest.”

The lab was a state of the art facility with special lighting and it had been built with all the latest biohazard security precautions. No windows to the outside, layers upon layers of security. She’d been inside for fourteen hours and hadn’t noticed.

“I’m so sorry, Dave!” She stood and buzzed the wolf she’d just spoken to. “Go home. I apologize, I didn’t realize it was so late. Please, next time just tell me if I’ve kept you here over twelve hours.”

Dr. Stewart, the other wolf, shook her head. “This is important. Really, please don’t apologize. I’m just glad you know so much about virology.”

“Me too. I had no idea that my fascination would actually be of such great use someday. Heck, I’m an ER doc, I sew people up, pull weapons out of them, set bones, that sort of thing. The lab stuff was sort of a weird hobby.”

They cleaned up, discarded their lab clothes and all headed out. She had two guards on her now. Cade insisted since she’d begun to work in the lab and he couldn’t be with her all day. She understood, he had his own work do to on Pack business and as a member of the Council of War.

“I’ll drive,” Dave said, opening her door. “You call Cade and let him know we’re on the way.”

Hiroshi, the other guard, sat on her other side in the back seat as Dave took them home. They were only ten minutes away but she pulled out her phone and called.

“You’d better be at the gates right now, Grace.”

“Fine way to answer the phone when your wife calls. We’re

leaving now and on the way. Do you want me to stop and pick anything up?"

"Have you eaten?"

"Um. Yes." At lunchtime.

"You forget I can feel you through the link even when you're miles away. When was the last time you ate?"

"You sound really tense. What's up? I'm sorry I'm so late in coming back. I just got caught up in this new strain."

His voice softened and his anger lessened through the link. "No, it's not you. I'll talk when you get here. I take it you haven't eaten since noon so I'll make us dinner and you'll eat it after a hot shower. I love you. Get home safe."

The rest of the ride went relatively quickly as she continued to work through the issues they faced with the virus.

Cade met them in the garage, sent Dave and Hiroshi to bed and escorted her to their bathroom. "Shower. I'll be in shortly with dinner so just get in bed." He kissed her softly and disappeared after turning on the water.

True to his word, when she emerged from the bathroom in a puff of steam, clean, warm and more relaxed, the scent of stew and fresh bread greeted her.

"You're so good to me." She crawled in bed and he tucked her in, putting a tray over her legs. She realized how hungry she was and wasted no time in getting started.

"Grace, you really shouldn't go so long without eating. You of all people should know how bad it is for your metabolism." Wolves had fast metabolisms. They needed about eight thousand calories a day to stay healthy and she'd not even gotten a third of that.

"I know. I didn't do it on purpose. I just got caught up. I want to talk to you about something but you need to tell me what's up first."

He put another big bowl of stew before her, removing the empty and slathering another slice of bread with butter before settling in next to her.

"There were more attacks today. A family in Northern California. Their five-year-old was beaten severely, the wife as well. The male and female managed to repel the attackers but he later died. In Charleston, a female was attacked in the parking lot of her bank. She's in serious condition but they think she'll pull through. Two attacks using silver injections. Both of those wolves died. There weren't any wolves nearby who were strong enough to bring their wolves to heal them. They died in human form."

Grace heard the pain in his voice. The pain of an Alpha whose people were suffering and he hadn't protected them. It didn't matter that they weren't Cascadia wolves. They were wolves. The Alpha and the doctor in Grace felt that pain. She put her tray on the floor next to the bed and snuggled into him, holding him tight.

"We need to get the word out about this silver dilution. And we need to find those labs."

"You know Ben and his people went into the lab location you gave us in Chicago. It was deserted but they couldn't take all the equipment so we were able to destroy it. Nina is providing some help with the computer stuff. Ben and Benoit are working together to find the other locations. You said there were several in Chicago. Lex may go out to help with tracking if they need him to. We're working with the Enforcer from Mid-States Pack and Eastern Seaboard on tracking labs there as well. Nashville seems to have a problem with your brother's people so they're concentrating there as well. Can you work on something to combat the silver in the lab?"

"We've tried for decades. The most effective thing we've found is to bring the wolf. Once it's in the bloodstream, it's fatal. Over half the time it's fatal even if we can bring the wolf. Dialysis would take too long and it's not convenient. If someone happened to be at a kidney center or a hospital with dialysis machines right when they were injected, it might work."

"I've advised Cascadia people who are farther out from this area to take their children and go away into the Clan haven. I don't know what else to do. I can't risk our children to a monster like Warren and his insanity." The haven was a failsafe, a bolt hole of sorts where the Pack would send the weakest members to safety. Children and their mothers came first and then the elderly.

She sighed and rubbed her hands up and down his back. Wishing she could comfort him more. "That's a good idea. You said the haven was the safest place and no one but you and Lex and the driver of the busses knew the exact location. That's for the best."

"I think you should go too."

She laughed. "Cade Warden! I'm Alpha of this Pack too. I don't run and hide. My place is at your side. Anyway, I'm needed here in the lab. I think we should move most of the personnel to creation of a vaccine. I've advised all but two people to move to that. We've got two of Warren's strains and the clean strain you had here before. I think that'll be enough to come up with something. I'm afraid if we don't we'll regret it."

"If you think it's a good idea, I trust your judgment. Let's talk to Lex, Ben and Jack tomorrow too. Will it work on humans?"

"I don't think so. The issue is what happens to wolves when given the virus. What it did to Gina, well, it was what it was because it forced her system to fight itself. It killed her immune system. Her cells disintegrated. What it's doing to humans, I can't deal with, with this vaccine. The problem is that there's been no effective cure or preventative inoculation against lycanthropy for humans. We've isolated the virus and your people have been working for nearly four years on this and haven't been able to find a solution. If we did human trials, it might work in a few years but with the escalating violence, the humans are even less inclined to work with us. We can't force it either. I'll speak with Benoit again, see if we can't get National's lab working on that aspect if we can drum up some volunteers."

"You're such a help to me. I wish..." he sighed, running his fingers through her hair, "...I wish we could just be together without any of this stuff. I just want things to be simple and peaceful. I want to lay around with you in bed all day. I hate the thought of you being in danger. I hate the thought of my niece and nephew being in danger, of the child Nina is carrying being in danger. I can't seem to stop it. Only you make it all right. You listen and you help. Thank you."

She hated that he was so pained, wished she could make it better for him. Wished she could get rid of her brother for him and make the world okay again.

"I'm glad. I want to love you, Cade. I want to be at your side and run this Pack. I want my brother gone."

"You're not going to work tomorrow until noon. It's a weekend and you're exhausted. For now, eat the rest of that food and then you're going to sleep. I'll ravish you in the morning."

She yawned and held him tighter, seeking and giving comfort. "I'm always for a good ravish."

Cade lay awake, cradling the most precious thing he'd ever seen in his arms. Worried. Upset. Satisfied. Overjoyed. Not all the wolves had openly accepted her. While she was their Alpha, they hadn't had the official ceremony to bring her into the Pack yet. That was planned for the next weekend. She held power over them but many distrusted her because of who she was. It had pissed him off to no end, but she'd simply accepted it and urged him to do the same.

Despite that rocky start, smudges of purpled exhaustion marked the skin beneath her eyes. She was at the lab twelve to fourteen hours every day and when she wasn't there she was at home working. On top of that, a few wolves had trusted her and began to seek her counsel about health-related problems.

But she hadn't been overwhelmed or annoyed by the added pressure. No, Grace had responded with joy and leadership, already making notes about the creation of a Cascadia walk-in-care clinic at the Pack house in Queen Anne.

She took her position seriously, which pleased him but also made him insane with worry. Several wolves who lived nearby had already spoken to him about sending their children and mates to the haven. He wished he had that option but knew she'd never do it, even as he suggested it to her earlier.

He supposed he wouldn't have respected her as much if she didn't insist on staying there at his side, but maybe not. Maybe he'd just be relieved instead of afraid of losing her.

Lex had already had an argument with Nina about it. Now that she was pregnant, he'd asked her to go to the haven with their grandmother. Both women simply looked at him as if he spoke gibberish. Damned female wolves. Smart and strong, capable.

He would have sighed but he didn't want to wake Grace up. He wanted her to be well rested when he took her the next morning.

Chapter Ten

"Can you think of anything else you may have forgotten about Warren? Anything at all?" Ben asked her over the phone. "Sometimes you may not think something is important but that one little thing is the key to helping us find the main lab or his headquarters."

Lex smoothed a hand up and down Grace's arm and Cade paced. They'd had zero luck in finding Warren's main lab.

She leaned forward and rubbed her forehead. "Why don't I come out there? I can drive around and see what I can find and remember?"

"No! It's too dangerous, Grace." Cade spun to look at her and she visibly counted to ten.

Grace stood. "Cade, may I speak to you outside, please?" Without waiting for an answer she left the room.

Cade looked to Lex and rolled his eyes heavenward. Grace had a fucking spine of steel. She chose her battles carefully and he'd noted that once she took a stand on something, he'd just as well kiss it goodbye. "Take over. I'll be right back."

Once he got to the end of the hall where she stood near the windows, sunlight backlighting her like a freaking angel, he nearly fell to his knees before her.

"I'm dead set against this, Grace."

"Cade, this is serious business. If we can find this damned lab we can make some serious strides toward taking him out once and for all. People are dying!"

There'd been more violence in the days following the last report. Groups of National Aligned Pack wolves were arming to the teeth and twice now, skirmishes had broken out with severe injuries and one death. Cade wasn't inclined to tell his people they couldn't defend themselves against the barbarism of Pellini. In fact, they'd been working with the Council of War to send Enforcer corps wolves, all specially trained, all over the country to the Pack seats of where clan resided, to protect their people. Some Packs had really well-trained Enforcers while others didn't. It was the time to pitch in and help.

"We can't just sit here while he does this, Cade. It's not what Alphas should do." Grace touched his neck. "I can't. If there's something that jogs my memory, I can't risk not going. You of all people should understand."

"Damn it, Grace. I can't leave right now. I have to meet with Pacific and Siskiyou tomorrow and the next day. Can't it wait until I can be there with you?"

"Cade, I rarely ask anything of you. But this is my job too and you know it. Let me do this. I'll go and come straight back in time for the ceremony this weekend. I'll take guards. Ben isn't going to let anything happen to me. Maxwell feels so guilty about shunning my family he's going to bend over backwards to keep me safe. Well, and keep from your wrath if anything did."

He pulled her to his body with a groan. "You're right, I know you are but I don't want to risk you. Grace, you're everything to me. I can't bear the thought of you being in danger."

"I know that. And I wouldn't do it if I didn't think it was necessary. But I can't live with myself if I don't do everything I can to stop this."

He growled. "Fine. Okay. But let's get a safety plan in place. If it's satisfactory I'll be more at ease although I want you to fly out and right back, all right?"

She nodded. "I don't want to be gone from you any longer than I have to either."

They went back into the room and Lex looked at his brother through hooded eyes. Both males knew the fear of losing a mate.

"I can't be there. Pacific and Siskiyou are expected here for a two day meeting and Lex is running training sessions for this expanded Enforcer corps. How can you keep Grace safe?" Cade grabbed Grace's hand and pulled her into his lap, holding her close. She snuggled into him and he rested his chin on the top of her head.

"I'll come out from Boston and meet her plane personally," Jack broke in. "I'll be her guard the whole time she's there. I'll even escort her home. You know I'll protect her with my life."

It was Jack's place as an anchor to step in and as the man was one of the most powerful wolves in the United States, the offer satisfied Cade.

"And as apparently I'm chopped liver, I'll also assign a team to her while she's here." Ben's voice was dry but Cade knew he got it. Tegan had nearly died, Ben would never forget it.

They made arrangements to have Grace's plane met first thing the next morning and for her to stay at Tegan and Ben's should she need to. Dave and Hiroshi would accompany her as well. He hated it but he knew she had to do it and if he stood in her way, he'd be robbing her of her rightful place and duty as Alpha. He knew Jack would protect her with his life. Knew his sister and Ben would as well. He'd never actually considered blowing off his responsibilities before, but he craved just tossing the meetings aside to go with her to Chicago. But she wouldn't have allowed it and he had too many lives in the balance to protect and think of.

Grace wandered out of the room when her part ended and all the Enforcer talk began. She itched to get back to the lab and work but knew when Cade finished up he'd come looking for her and be upset if she was gone.

She didn't relish the idea of going to Chicago again either.

"Hey, you all right?" Nina came down the stairs. "How about a cup of tea? By the look on your face, I bet Cade will be baking soon. Well—" she looked Grace up and down, "—after the sexin'."

Grace followed Nina into the kitchen and made her sit while she took over the tea preparation. A commotion sounded downstairs and suddenly a goofy-looking three-legged dog bounded into the room, heading straight for her.

"Milton!"

To keep from landing on her butt in the middle of the kitchen floor in a heap of goofy-looking three-legged dog, Grace put her arms around the dog to steady them both. He gave a happy groan and licked her face.

"Get off her. That's an Alpha you're licking all over." Milton was pulled back and his face was replaced by the freckled, green-eyed woman with an eyebrow ring who must have owned him. "Hi, you're Grace I wager. I'm Tracy."

Before Grace could speak, she was enveloped in a hug from the only one of her sisters-in-law she hadn't met yet.

"Whoo, hot werewolf alert. Hiya big guys."

Grace looked around Tracy to see what Nina was talking about and saw her assessment of hotness was pretty darned correct. As they were most likely her brothers-in-law and Tracy's mates, she looked back to Tracy.

"It's nice to finally meet you. Oh and Milton. I've heard a lot about him." She scratched behind his ear and he made that groan again.

"You must be popular with all the guys with those hands." Tracy winked and turned to Nina. "My God, Nina, you weren't kidding, she's like, teeny." And back to Grace again. "You're very teeny. I feel like a heifer next to you. I'm going to sit next to Nina."

"Thanks very much," Nina said dryly. "Oh the eye candy over here? The one in the thousand dollar suit is Nick Lawrence and the one who looks like that hot professor you had dirty fantasies about is Gabe Murphy. Guys, this is Grace."

"Grace who is getting a complex with all the comments about how tiny she is. Welcome to you, it's very nice to meet all three of you. I was just about to make some tea, would you like some? Or something else?" All these giant males were positively oozing testosterone and it made her itchy to grab Cade and shove him against something.

"They're in the office on a phone call with the Council if you're interested." Nina waved in the direction of the office.

Gabe nodded, kissed Tracy and turned to Grace. He took her hand and bowed, giving her a courtly kiss. "It's a pleasure to meet you, as well, Grace. What you've done takes a lot of courage and character. It's an honor to have you in the family."

"Really, it's nothing. Not compared to what you all do." She blushed and Nick chuckled.

"Don't be silly. I know how hard it is to deal with your family when they're up to no good. But you risked your life to get us this information. That's something. I know you haven't been accepted on all fronts because of your brother but you're always welcome in Pacific territory and I'm proud we're related," Nick said.

"Thank you."

"Go on, you're making her blush." Tracy swatted Nick's butt playfully and he winked at them and followed Gabe down the hall toward the office.

"Now, you were about to tell me what the hell is in the air." Nina gave her a pointed look as she poured the hot water in the pot to steep.

"First, eat something. Here, pumpkin bread. I made it last night. Cade ate almost all of it but I held some back for you." She put a plate in front of Nina and brought some extra out for Tracy as well.

She told them about the trip to Chicago.

"Wow. I imagine there'll be loads of cookies to eat now. Cade must have flipped." Nina forked some of the bread into her mouth.

Grace put out cups for the tea. "He's upset. I would be in his place. I am actually. I don't, well, I don't have fond memories of Chicago. I'm not anxious to go back."

Tracy sat back in her chair. Megan came in, gave her sister a hug and joined them, pouring out tea. Unshed tears stung the back of Grace's eyes. Family. She'd never had that with her biological family. She'd had it with wolves from Great Lakes but then lost it. In that moment as the four of them ate and shared their troubles, the fact that she hadn't had that support in years nearly knocked the breath from her.

Megan touched her shoulder. "Are you all right, Grace?"

The door down the hall slammed open and footsteps sounded as Cade rushed into the kitchen. He knelt at her side. "Honey, what is it? Are you all right?"

She sniffled, hating to be the center of attention. Damn that link sometimes. "I'm fine. I just remembered for a moment. Go back to your meeting."

He leaned in and kissed her face, taking her tears into his mouth. "Remembered what?"

"What it was like before you. Before this." She indicated the table, her sisters-in-law. "I didn't have this. It was very lonely. But now I do and despite the war, despite the threat of violence, I've never been so happy. I know that's selfish."

Suddenly she was surrounded by many arms and even a cold, wet dog nose pressed into her leg. Surrounded by love and understanding. It comforted her but the bittersweetness was sharp and her tears flowed openly.

Cade felt her pain through the link and moved to her, not caring about what was being said. She needed him, he felt it and he'd provide what she needed.

Feeling her break this way, really truly feeling the depth of her loneliness of her life before he'd met her devastated him. Because he'd been in Seattle with his family. Loving them and being loved. Knowing always that he had a place in the world that was his.

And she hadn't. When she'd been shunned along with the rest of the Pellinis she'd lost her place, that assurance she belonged. It would have been easy to overlook what the rest of them did, to overlook it and have a place among her own people. To wolves, being among Pack was second nature. It fed heart and mind and she'd shunned it because it was the right thing to do.

Admiration swelled deep along with his love for her. Seeing other wolves with their mates, he'd felt envy but knowing her then, knowing she was made just for him, knowing his soul was worthy of a woman like Grace? It made him a better man, strengthened his faith that this standoff with Warren Pellini and his thugs was going to end with them victorious and the threat Pellini posed to their race erased forever.

"Okay, tea is ready. Why don't you go back to your meeting, Cade? We're going to have some girl talk, feed Milton tofu corn dogs and gossip about you guys and your sexual prowess." Nina smiled at him over the top of Grace's head.

Grace's tears turned into a snort of laughter and he kissed her, needing a taste.

"Are you going to be all right?"

"Yes. I told you that already. Go on and work. We'll talk when you're finished."

"We'll do more than that. Just a warning." He stood, happy at the way she ducked her head and blushed. He trusted his sisters to help and reach out. He'd do the rest with Grace at his side.

Grace smiled as she washed up. Girl talk was something she'd missed a great deal and her sisters-in-law were really enjoyable people. Tracy was a lot like Nina, if the world could actually handle two of them. Megan was more like Grace but still had a dry, sharp wit. She was also lonely. Grace knew it, saw the same look in her eyes that had greeted her in the mirror every morning before Cade Warden had touched her that very first time.

Layla had stopped in as well to see Tracy, she probably enjoyed Layla the most of all the sisters-in-law. The woman was secure in her own skin, observant, funny, a great mother and Grace loved to watch her interact with her husband, Sid. The tall, lanky artist looked at Layla like she hung the moon. The two were total opposites and yet they worked on a level Grace only hoped she and Cade would eleven years down the line.

"Hey there. Need any help?"

She turned to watch Cade enter the room with that predator's walk of his. Just the sight of him, all coiled up, the ease over the steely resolve, made her mouth dry up. God, he was sexy. So sexy it overwhelmed her at times. Never in her existence had she obsessed about sex but with him, she craved it every moment of the day. He brought out desires she'd never imagined much less given even an inner voice to. And he did it all with total ease.

"My goodness, whatever are you thinking about, Grace Warden? The blast of what you just sent through the link has made me very, very hard." He backed her against the counter and ground his cock into her. An involuntary gasp came from within and she clutched at his upper arms.

"You," she whispered. "Always you, Cade."

"I love it when you look at me like this. Like you want to eat me up and lick your lips afterward."

His hands roamed all over her body and she closed her eyes, luxuriating in his touch. "I love it when you touch me like that. Like I'm so precious you're afraid I'll break but you can't help yourself."

She opened her eyes to find his just inches away as he bent down to kiss the tip of her nose. "I can't help myself, Grace. But you're so small, so important and such a miracle to me I'm afraid you'll disappear like smoke in the night."

"I'm wearing three-inch heels," she said, losing a bit of breath as he kissed the spot just below her ear.

"And you're still small. But I *like* that. You make me calm just by thinking of you. Well, you make me want to fuck you every time I think of you too. But my point is, you're regal and cool and petite but you take up every part of me. Your wolf is amazing, just like you are. I'm this big lumbering fool and you're this pixie and yet, you're mine." He shrugged and she smiled, reaching up to run her hands through his hair. Loving the way he felt.

"I am. And you're mine. Don't you let that hussy from Siskiyou flirt while I'm not here. Don't think I haven't noticed how she bats her eyelashes at you." Heifer.

He chuckled and suddenly her blouse was open, his hands on her breasts. "God, I love that you're bare under your blouses. Drives me nuts to see you walking around. Does it feel good, Grace? The cool fabric against your nipples?"

"Anyone could walk in here," she said, not convincingly.

"They could. And you didn't answer my question. Sometimes I see you move and your nipples press against the fabric and my response is Pavlovian. My mouth waters, my tongue wants to swirl around your nipple until you make that squeak. The honey will make your pussy all slick and ready for me."

"Yes," she whispered as she blushed. He made her bold.

"Yes your cunt gets wet when my mouth is on your nipple? Yes your nipples feel good against your shirt?"

"Yes to both." Little zings of pleasure rebounded through her system as his lips skated down her neck, all the while his fingers plucked at her nipples.

He dropped to his knees and his mouth went to one nipple and then the other, over and over. People were still there, downstairs and outside. She was torn between the thrill of possibly being discovered and the possible embarrassment.

His hands slid up her bare legs, up beneath the hem of her skirt. She squirmed and he pressed against her with his upper body, holding her in place. The blunt pads of his fingers brushed over the lace of her panties and he hummed his pleasure.

"Wet. Soaking wet for me. I'm going to make you come right here, Grace. Right here when anyone could walk in and catch me licking your succulent nipples and fingering your pussy. And you're going to love it. You *do* love it. The scent of your cunt drives me insane. I can smell you now, smell how much you want me."

He pushed aside the crotch of her underwear and slid his fingers into the wet folds of her pussy. She widened her legs as she bit her bottom lip to keep from crying out. His tongue flicked over her nipple, his fingers, two of them, slid into her gate while his thumb pressed insistently over her clit.

She locked her knees to keep standing, gripped the counter behind her. Her head fell back as she breathed through her nose, struggled to not scream her pleasure as he played her body expertly. He moved his mouth to the other nipple as his other hand slid through her pussy and back. Slick with her honey, his middle finger stroked over her rear passage, sending taboo arcs of electric sensation through her.

"I'm going to put my cock here, Grace. When you get off that plane tomorrow night, we're coming back here and I'm going to fuck your ass." The finger he'd been sliding back and forth penetrated just a bit and she gasped. "Mmm, no one's been back there, have they?"

"No," she managed to say.

"Good."

He bit down, taking in as much of her breast as he could and worked his magic with his fingers. Ribbons of color streaked her vision until orgasm hit and her entire body tightened with the pressure to keep quiet.

She dimly felt him put her panties and skirt in place. He picked her up and walked her toward their part of the house.

Cade's entire body vibrated with need. The way she'd responded as he'd spoken of taking her ass had nearly broken him. Her cunt had heated even more than usual, spilling that ultra-hot juice on his hands. Fuck she was hot and she didn't even realize her power. God help him if she ever did. She'd own him.

"Undress, Grace. I need to be inside you. I need to mark you before you hie off on this insane trip to Chicago." He ripped off his shirt, the buttons flying, never taking his eyes from her.

Sex tousled, that's what she was. Her movements were fluid, but slower than normal, her eyes half lidded. He could scent her, knew she was in a state of satiation but also need. Knew she needed this physical connection as much as he did.

Pride. Satisfaction that he made this woman feel so good, feel such need to be with him, roared through his system.

Bit by bit, her pretty skin was revealed to his eyes until she lay there, totally naked, watching his body as he undressed as well.

"You're amazing. I've seen beefcake pictures in the magazines and they've got nothing on you."

He grinned, loving the way she looked at him. He felt eight feet tall and centerfold handsome when her attention was on him.

"Looking at beefcake in magazines, huh?" He got on the bed and crawled over her body. "Should I be jealous?"

His skin tingled where she skimmed her palms up the muscles of his back.

"No. There's no room for anything or anyone else now that you're mine." Such a simple statement and yet it knocked him out.

"I need you, Grace."

"Then take me. I'm yours." Those amber eyes looked up into his face, trusting him with her body and soul, humbling him.

With their difference in height, it wasn't easy to take her from above unless he was on his knees so he arranged himself and she automatically wrapped her thighs around his waist, scooting close.

"You already know me so well."

She laughed, he loved the sound.

"Well it's not like it's a mystery. The parts go where they go."

"Oh like, here?" he asked as he slid deep into her pussy.

Her intake of breath seemed to draw the walls of her cunt in tighter around him, even as the creamy flesh parted for him, making room, welcoming him home.

"Christ. Each time I tell myself I'm going to go slow. That I'll take my time and draw out the experience but once my cock slices into your pussy, that all falls away and I want to rut on you, in you."

She blushed, blinking quickly. "I...when you say that sort of thing, it makes me breathless. I've never thought of being that sort of woman to any man. I'm wildly flattered. It makes me very happy."

He petted down her flanks and then back over her belly and across the closely trimmed curls at the base of her mound. With a growl, he changed his tempo, speeding up, fucking into her body in short, feral digs.

Her scent changed subtly, heated, sweetened. Her nipples drew tight and darkened against the surrounding lighter pink. He wanted that moment to freeze, wanted to never forget the beauty of her response to him, the way she opened up her normally reserved personality and luxuriated in the sensuality that lay just beyond—just for him. *Only for him.*

"Will you touch yourself for me? Make yourself come, Grace."

Her breath caught but the flood of moisture around his cock told him she wasn't bothered by the idea at all. Fuck. He tried to think of the table of elements to keep from coming but he was close.

"I want to see you."

She nodded, her hand sliding down her belly. Her fingers brushed against his cock, down where their bodies joined, gathering moisture and taking it back to her clit. He sat back straighter so he could watch.

The pale skin of her hand stood in stark contrast to the darkened flesh of her pussy, glistening with her lube. His cock thrust into her and pulled back out, her body loath to let him go.

Her eyelids sank as her lips parted.

"Jesus you're so hot. So sexy. Look at me, I want to look into your eyes when you come, when I come inside you."

Slowly, she dragged her eyes open and continued to finger her clit, her body tightening around his. She hissed and arched as her pussy clamped down around his cock. It was all he could take and with a long groan he thrust deep and came.

Their eyes never left each other. He felt her within him, where she'd been lodged since the first time he got a good whiff of her two weeks prior.

Without a word, he carried her into their bathroom and ran the water. He needed to minister to her, the way she had him countless times since he'd claimed her.

Chapter Eleven

He'd been so good to her the night before after making love. He'd taken her to their shower and washed her hair, soaped up her body as she stood under the warm spray and let him do all the work.

She'd marveled out loud to him of his sweetness as she'd sighed, leaning back into his body as he soaped up her hair. His hands on her scalp had been strong but gentle.

He'd looked at her like she was the most precious thing he'd ever seen and said, "I'm in love with you. I want to take care of you. You've been working so hard, I just want to send you off to Chicago with my hands on you in your memory."

And they'd been. The way he'd kneaded her neck as they'd rejoined the rest of the family for wine out on the deck. The way he'd looked at her in the moonlight as if no one and nothing else existed.

All her life, despite being the smart one, the overachiever, the successful one, she'd never actually felt cherished and adored. He did that.

So she could get on that plane before the sun rose and head to Chicago to do her best because he made her want to be the best person she could.

"You're good for him," Dave said from his seat across from her. "For a long time all that existed for Cade was the Pack. He became more and more obsessed with details and control and less warm. Less human and more wolf I suppose. The difference is amazing. The Cade I grew up with is back."

"I feel like I'm in a fairy tale, you know? He takes care of me, he worries about me. He makes me eat my vegetables and counts my calories to be sure I eat enough." She shrugged with a smile. Cade made her want to cry sometimes and it wasn't something she normally did.

Dave moved next to her and put his arm around her, smoothing a hand over her hair. The strength of Pack, the love of Pack. He knew her, knew she needed the touch and gave it. No judgment, just love.

They landed and true to his word, Jack met her right at the stairs of the plane with a big hug and a kiss on the top of her head.

"Hey there, shortstuff." He handed her a cup of coffee and a brown paper bag. "Coffee and a bagel, cheese, meat thing."

She grinned. "Thank you, Jack."

All the while, he'd been hustling her to the car where Tegan waited inside. Dave sat up front with the driver and Ben sat just behind them with Benoit.

Tegan rubbed her face along Grace's jaw. "Morning, Grace."

Grace greeted them all, took a sip of coffee and called the house to let Cade know she'd arrived safely. He insisted on talking to Jack, who humored him and promised to keep her safe before hanging up.

"Okay, head out to the area around the lab you found Tegan at. I've been thinking about it for a bit and wondering. When we were kids, my parents had this restaurant we used to go to. It's not there anymore. I can't remember exactly where it was but I looked around online and I think it may be around there."

They headed out and she sat back in the seat and tried to think. She hadn't met Warren at Pellini Group headquarters. She'd met him again after arranging it through their parents. She'd tried to contact them since she'd left Chicago but they'd changed their number and Ben told her they'd cleared out of their house leaving nothing behind. Both of them worked for her brother in some capacity so there wasn't a job she could trace them to.

There had to be a key, something she was overlooking.

"You looked at my condo?" she asked absently, leaning into Jack.

"We did. They'd been there. Kicked your door in. I'm sorry to say your stuff had been totally wrecked. We got a scent trail but lost it a few blocks away. They'd been to your old job as well but since you left and cut off contact with everyone so long ago, no one knew anything." Ben had leaned forward to answer her and she reached back to touch him. She realized the way they were Pack and it warmed her.

Tegan smiled when she caught her eye, a knowing smile. Grace knew her sister-in-law had had her own share of heartache but had found something special with Ben. Still, even as she'd been hurting, she'd been surrounded by Wardens. Not such a bad thing.

"So how's it going? How are the wolves in the Pack accepting you?" Tegan asked.

"It's getting better slowly I think. At first no one trusted me. Now it's just most of the Pack who don't trust me." It hurt but she knew why. Her brother had harmed so many.

"They suck. You want me to kill anyone for you, shortstuff?" Jack's voice rumbled in her ear.

She laughed. "I think I'll be all right. They just have to get to know me. I know why they feel the way they do. Warren has sent them all into upheaval. He nearly killed Tegan, he brought war to their lives."

"You're not him."

She felt Jack's fierce anger and realized they had a link too. Not as strong as what she felt with Cade, but it was there.

"I hate that you're being punished when you're so damned brave. You did the right thing. Hell you did something most people would never have the guts to do. How dare they judge you."

She turned and looked at Jack. "They're afraid."

"Of you?"

"Of everything. My brother has turned their lives upside down. He's taken the very thing that makes them what they are and is using that against them. I understand why they don't like me. I understand why they don't trust me. Obviously I hope they'll change their minds when they get to know me. But they have a lot at risk just now."

"You have more at risk, damn it." Jack frowned and she reached up to smooth away the lines on his forehead, realizing now, a bit of how Nina must have felt for Cade.

"Life isn't fair, Jack. Didn't your mother ever tell you that?"

He laughed. "Yeah. All the time. She still tells me."

They rolled up into the neighborhood where the old lab had been and got out. Jack growled and kept her in his shadow the whole time while Dave got her other side and Hiroshi stood just behind them. Ben had two other wolves with him as well as Tegan and Agent Benoit just stood back and let them work.

"You don't have to stand on top of me. None of you are going to be able to scent anything with everyone so close." Grace sighed. "And I can't scent anything either. For that matter, I can't *see* anything because as everyone loves to remind me, I'm short and you're all huge."

Jack and Dave still stayed close but everyone else backed off a bit as they walked through the surrounding neighborhoods. She just sort of turned off her brain and wandered. Her link to her family still existed somewhere within her. She just needed to find it and try to keep it one way. She often did mindless tasks when she worked through a problem. She'd come up with some of her best ideas when ironing and folding laundry. Just walking, letting the sounds around her lull her brain seemed to help guide her.

She turned left and walked for several blocks and turned again. On and on it went. They'd been walking for several hours and had entered residential neighborhoods and commercial zones and back again but kept going, giving Grace the lead.

Ben had long since transformed into a wolf and when he growled softly, everyone halted, noses in the air.

"I want you off the street, Grace. Now." Jack pulled her toward the SUV that'd been following a few blocks behind.

"What? Why? I...this may be somewhere important. It feels..."

He literally picked her up and put her in the car and the breath whooshed out of her. Dave gave him a look but said nothing as he slid in beside them.

"It feels dangerous for a group of werewolves to be walking around sniffing the air. You're royalty, Grace, don't you forget. We can't take a chance at being made and by having us all out there like that, we endangered everyone including you. Especially you. Your brother demanded your return. Did you know that?"

Dave put his face in his hands.

"What? No. How long ago?"

"Wait. Something is happening." Jack looked past her.

They all looked out the windows to see the group circling back.

"Go back to the lab. Ben and Hiroshi will meet us there." Tegan got into the car and belted in.

"Now you can tell me what the hell you meant about Warren demanding I be returned to him. Like a pair of shoes or something?"

"Cade didn't tell you? Shit. Well, he deserves the ass kicking then. I told him to tell you. Yes. When you went to Seattle with Cade, Warren called us first. His people had gone to your condo, saw some of your things gone and scented Great Lakes wolves had been there. Maxwell told him you'd mated with Cade and had joined Cascadia. Warren flipped. Demanded your return and then threatened to send his people to grab you back, said you'd been taken illegally. Maxwell said, even if you had been, Warren was a lawbreaker and in no position to demand satisfaction because he was marked for death anyway. He said you were marked for death and Maxwell told him if he even so much as breathed in your direction every wolf in the National Pack Alliance would come down on his head and rip him to pieces." Tegan looked out the window and Grace realized she was worried about Ben.

"I can't believe Cade didn't tell me that. But enough for now on that. What's going on?"

"I think Ben smelled something. Hiroshi too. They'll change at the lab and we'll hear then. It felt different when we went down that last block."

Jack looked at Tegan and nodded. "It did. We may have been watched."

They pulled up at the lab and Hiroshi and Ben jumped in.

"Go," Ben barked and they sped away.

“What the hell is going on?” Grace demanded.

“You’re going back to Seattle right now. There are Pellini wolves in that neighborhood. I don’t know if we’ve been made or not but I need to run him to ground and you need to be out of the fucking state when I do it or Cade will personally kill me.” Ben got on the phone and began to order people around on the other end. Benoit did the same and Grace sighed.

“This is stupid. I can help.” Grace said it knowing it was useless.

“Don’t cross your arms over your chest and look stubborn. You *have* helped. We wouldn’t have walked through every neighborhood in a fifteen-mile radius just sniffing the air. Who’d have thought your brother would be holed up in some blue-collar neighborhood? I’d have pegged him for a mansion like your parents lived in,” Tegan said. “You did your part, Grace. Now it’s our turn. Heavily armed, specially trained people need to do this.”

“No arguments, Grace. I’m taking you back like I promised.” Jack ignored her pout and they headed straight for the airport where they shoved her on a plane, she ordered them to stay safe and they took off.

“Are you hungry, Grace?” Dave asked as they reached safe altitude to move around.

“Yes. Yes I am. Shall I help you make something?”

“Sit and let me help for a change. The galley should be well stocked. Cade called ahead yesterday.” Dave went to the back of the jet and Grace slid her shoes off and tucked her feet beneath her.

“Are you all right?” Jack asked.

“Worried about them. My brother is unstable. Dangerous. If something happens to any of them—” She broke off, unable to even contemplate how Cade and the others would react.

"It's our job. It's what an Enforcer does, Grace. Ben is specially trained as a cop, Tegan has been in the Enforcer corps since she was barely out of her teens. All those wolves back there know their shit. Your brother has to be taken out, there's simply no other way at this point. Benoit said a human was caught in the crossfire between wolves. That sort of thing puts us all in even more danger. If humans get involved, we're in big trouble."

Dave brought back a big tray filled with food and they all tucked in and ate. She was tired and worried but she knew to eat or Cade would be upset and it wouldn't do her any good to let herself get worn down.

Afterward, Jack had put a blanket over her and pulled her against him. "Rest now. We've got hours to go yet."

It wasn't as hard as she'd thought to fall asleep surrounded by Dave and Jack's scent.

Lex paced at the private airfield. Anxiety rode his nerves and he wasn't sure what it was. His people had gone over the field an hour before and all was clear. It was probably Nina. She'd been pissed off that he'd made her stay back at the house. Could be his brother too. Cade was livid but Lex had refused to let his brother come to get Grace. Two Alphas at the airfield in a time of war? Absurd. And there was the little fact of hello, Lex Warden, big bad Enforcer?

"Megan, you there?" he asked into the wrist mic.

"I'm here." He'd stationed her at the other end of the field to keep an eye on things. She had a good eye, one of the very few people he trusted totally.

"Something feel off to you?"

"Yes. But I've checked in with everyone and so far so good. I'm sure it's just the stress of not hearing back from Tee yet."

The control tower let them know the plane would be landing momentarily and they moved back as the sleek, small jet taxied down the runway and came to a halt.

He saw Dave come down the steps followed by Jack and then a glimpse of Grace and Hiroshi after her. Breathing sigh of relief, he motioned to have the car brought close and walked to greet them.

He wasn't able to stop his grin at the sight of his sister-in-law. So serious, intellectual and compassionate, but she had a quirky sense of humor and God knew she adored Cade and she kept Nina in line, which he had to admire in a big way.

"Okay, everyone can let me go now." She tried to get around them to move toward the car but looked up to see Lex and smiled. "Hey, any news?"

He put an arm around her and kissed the top of her head. "Nothing. But they had to plan and get ready. Lots of humans in the area so they're probably just watching and waiting for dark."

He opened the door and that's when he heard it.

Jack had too and shoved her down, landing on top of her. A helicopter had dropped three wolves carrying automatic weapons onto the tarmac and as they ran toward the car, they shot.

"Get her in the car, now!" Lex screamed and Jack moved faster than any wolf Lex had ever seen. In one deft toss, Grace landed in the car and Jack slammed the door, staying just outside.

Megan came running and in a moment of utter unreality, Lex watched a bloom of red cover her chest. She looked down and then fell. Lex transformed and charged their attackers as his own people came from all corners of the airfield, shooting, growling, transforming.

"Oh my God!" Grace shoved at Jack to get out but he held her there as she watched Megan get shot. She realized it was their normal car and she rifled under the seat until she found her traveling bag, just a basic medical bag but she thanked the heavens she'd been compulsive enough to carry it everywhere before going out the other door and running around the back of the car toward Megan.

Dave saw her and moved to grab her as Jack growled her name and charged. But she was an Alpha, damn it, she was fast and powerful and she would not let anyone but her brother's people die out there that day. She jumped around Dave who knocked into the last standing attacker. The wet sounds of teeth meeting flesh and strangled cries sounded in her ears right as the white-hot pain of a bullet ripped through her chest.

But she kept moving until she reached Megan.

"Megan, honey, you have to change. You have to. I can't help you. Not like this." She leaned down and spoke in her sister-in-law's ear. "The wound is too much. You can't heal as a human. Come on, I order you to change, damn it. Bring your wolf, Megan. Come on!"

Her fingers were slick with blood as she grabbed Megan to hold her close. She realized it was her own as her left arm began to go numb.

"Grace! Fuck, fuck. You've been shot. Damn it, why didn't you stay put?" Jack reached her and fell to his knees. "Come on. Come on, let's get out of here."

She turned to him and snarled. "I'm not going anyfuckingwhere! This is my sister, she's my wolf and she has to change or she will die. You will help me bring her wolf and you'll do it now. LEX!" she screamed and Lex approached, naked from his shift back to human form. Grief on his face when he saw Megan.

"Shit, Grace, you're... No, not both of you. Get in the car or I will put you in the trunk."

"We're wasting time! Bring her wolf! She can be healed if we bring her wolf. NOW. Damn it, now."

And the whip crack of authority in her voice finally made them hear her. Both men looked to Megan who barely breathed and began to chant at her, put their hands on her, ordered her wolf to emerge.

And then in a shower of power, weak and warm but there nonetheless, Megan found her wolf.

"Get her into the car and back to the house now." Grace stood and fell to her knees.

"Hospital." Jack picked her up and Lex his sister and they jumped into the car.

"No. Not the hospital. They'll have to make a police report. We can't risk any more exposure. Take me home. I have medical supplies there, I've stored them just in case. Let me transform once I know Megan is all right. For now..." she paused as more blood pulsed from the wound just inches above her heart, "...the bullet passed through. Silver. Tear strips from your shirt and pack the wound. I'm losing blood." The Pack doctor had headed to the haven as there were several pregnant women who needed her care. Grace had to stay human until she knew all was well.

Dave drove the car faster than was totally safe but Hiroshi kept an eye out for anyone following and called ahead to the house.

Grace slumped back into Jack, feeling his anxiety and worry for her. "Grace, you have to be all right. Change now."

She shook her head. “Can’t. If I do, I may be too weak to change right back. If Megan needs me…”

She lapsed in and out of consciousness. A normal bullet and her metabolism would already be healing but the silver, even just passing through was poisoning her, impeding healing.

“Cade is going to rip my head off.” Lex brushed the hair away from her face. “You were hell on wheels out there today, Grace. You saved Megan’s life. But if you ever disobey like that again, I’m gonna kick that tiny little ass.”

“And whose army?”

“You shouldn’t let her hang around Nina so much,” Dave called from the front seat. “We’re here. Hold on, they’re opening the gates for us now.”

“Megan on the low table in the living room. Bring my supplies.” Grace had to do that one last thing and then she could transform.

She heard Hiroshi relay the order and allowed herself to rest again. It began to hurt to breathe and she figured there was internal bleeding to deal with as well.

They skidded to a stop and the doors yanked open. Cade. The scent of Cade rushed through her system as Jack got out, still holding her.

“What the fuck? Whose blood is that?” Cade demanded in the background. They apparently hadn’t told him, which was wise. Hiroshi began to explain as Jack followed Lex and took them into the living room. She heard Cade’s bellow of anger in the background.

People rushed around Megan but Grace pushed them back until she could ascertain Megan was all right. Her breathing was normal as was her blood pressure. Grace turned in slow motion to see Cade, throwing aside the wolves who’d been trying to hold him back while she did her check. She coughed and wiped a hand over her lips, staining her skin scarlet. Lovely.

"Okay," she whispered and fell to her knees. Cade surrounded her, crying out her name as she let her wolf take over.

Cade saw her as the car door opened and Jack stepped out, holding her. Her entire left side was covered in blood. He remembered thinking Megan must have lost a lot of blood. He'd felt pain through the link and weakness but he hadn't figured... Hers, the blood was hers.

He found himself surrounded by wolves as they rushed past him into the house. Dave explained what had happened, told him he needed to hold back until they knew Megan was all right so Grace would allow her wolf to take over so she could heal.

He'd run to follow, screaming her name, feeling her through their link weaker and weaker. They held him as she checked Megan, his family anxious, wanting her to finish up for Megan and Grace's sake. He'd tossed off five wolves and finally reached her just as she wiped her hand over her face, smearing blood over her terribly pale skin.

Terror like he'd never felt took hold of him and they were surrounded, surrounded by Pack as they lent love and touch and she'd changed. He'd found himself cradling her wolf, the small, honey-gold wolf that held his mate's heart and soul.

He'd put his face to her fur and wept.

Chapter Twelve

Grace woke up, naked and wrapped up in hard, male werewolf. Another hard, male werewolf opened his eyes and looked at her. Blue as the summer sky.

Behind her, Cade startled awake and sat up. Jack looked to him. "Our girl is awake."

She turned to Cade and watched as the worry etched his forehead. "Honey? Are you all right? How are you feeling?" He ran his hands all over her body and despite her state of health, she responded quite resoundingly.

"Well, um, you're going to embarrass me if you don't stop that," she said, reaching up to take his hand and bring it to her lips.

"You do smell much better aroused than at death's door, Grace. And don't be embarrassed on my account." Jack spoke in the background. "I'm going to go and let everyone know you're awake. I'll do my best to stop a stampede."

She heard the door close and looked back to Cade. "I'm all right."

"You nearly died, Grace. You disobeyed your Enforcer and put yourself right in harm's way and today you are going to the haven. Period."

She sat up and put pillows at her back. "I will do no such thing. And I don't take orders not to save my wolves so fuck right off."

His eyes widened. "Did you just say fuck?"

"I'm not a precious little princess, Cade Warden. I can say the big bad words when they're called for and being told to sit by when one of my wolves is bleeding to death on the asphalt just ten feet away from me is one of those occasions. Oh and I'm not going to the haven so forget that right now."

"You would have died if you hadn't changed into a wolf right when you did." His widened eyes then narrowed with frustration.

"So used to being obeyed, aren't you?" She kissed the hand she still held. "Well tough. I'm the doctor here. I had about three more minutes before I would have lost consciousness and most likely died either from my lungs, which were pretty messed up, or blood loss. But I didn't die. Now, how is Megan and have you heard anything from Chicago?"

He got off the bed and brought back a shirt, which he put on over her head. "People are going to be in here any second and I don't want them to see your beautiful breasts. They're all mine." He tucked the blankets around her and as he got back onto the bed next to her, Megan opened the door and rushed inside, tears in her eyes.

"Thank God you're all right. You saved my life, Grace. You risked your own to save me. I can't even..." She lost her words on tears.

"You're my wolf. My family. I love you and I'd die for you. You have to know that. Not that I planned to get shot in the chest, let's be clear, I wasn't showing off or anything. How are you?" Grace took her pulse and looked into her eyes until Cade cleared his throat.

"Sit your pretty little butt back down. She's fine. It's been a day. She went for a run earlier this morning and was able to transform back a few hours ago. You transformed back into human form last night but stayed asleep. I spoke with the Pack doctor and she said to leave you that way so we did." Cade pulled her against his body and she let herself melt into him.

"Chicago?"

"Pushy. They found your brother's house, their Pack house. He was gone. They did apprehend several wolves though and Ben is questioning them. They also found the viral stores, Grace. They're destroyed now and the data is being couriered here by hand. I figured it would be helpful."

She tried to sit again and Cade merely tightened his arms to keep her in place. "What? You can't tell me you have all this info on the way and then not let me get to the lab to make ready for it."

"Oh but I can. That's what's so cool about being Alpha and all. The best thing is that you're still too weak to fight me on it just yet. I'll get you to the lab when the time is right. But for now, keep that pretty little ass right here in bed."

"Enough of that, you two. Let's get you fed. You need to get your strength back up." Tracy pushed into the room holding a tray and put it over her legs. "Thank you, Grace." Tracy kissed her cheek. "You saved my sister's life. You were a true Alpha out there."

"You honor me. Anyway, no harm. I'm all right. Megan let me examine her and I feel much better. What's the status of all the Great Lakes wolves?" She bit into the warm meatloaf and instantly began to feel better.

Cade sighed. "Two of Ben and Tegan's Enforcers were injured, one severely. But no deaths. No sign of your parents either. Now eat, damn it. You don't have a single ounce extra on you to fritter away. Everyone else needs to get out so you can rest."

"I'd like to speak to Jack and Lex please," she said around a mouthful of potatoes au gratin. "Who made this? It's really good."

"Thank you, pretty. It's an old bachelor recipe." Gabe smiled at her, kissed the top of her head and nodded to Cade. "Shall I take up with the meetings?"

"You've delayed them all this time? Cade, go on. I'm fine."

Cade looked to Gabe. "I'll be there in about an hour. Can you send Lex and Jack this way in about half an hour please?"

Once everyone had filed out and Grace's belly was full and round like a melon, she sat back with a sigh.

"Don't you ever, *ever fucking do that again.*" Cade's wolf flashed in his eyes. "Do you know what it felt like? Seeing you there? Watching you *die?* Because I won't do it again. Ever. Damn you for getting out of that car. Damn you for not changing on the way back once Megan had transformed. Why did you wait?"

She turned and straddled his lap, curling into him like a kitten. "In the first place, I'm sorry. I am. I can't imagine but the idea of seeing you that way makes me sick to my stomach. I didn't do it on purpose. It wasn't like I planned it but she was out there all alone. Bleeding out. Your sister was dying because she tried to protect me and I'm a doctor! I'm her Alpha and it was my duty and one I did without hesitation. And I'd do it again. I waited because I wanted to be sure she survived the transformation. I knew once I changed I'd be out and if she needed me once we got here to the house and I was a wolf, how could I help? You'd have done it. I didn't do it to be heroic or anything like that. I did it because it's what I needed to do. I'd be pissed if you did it too, I'll say that up front. I'm into equal opportunity hypocrisy. But I want you to understand I didn't do it to be flip and I did it knowing I was taking a chance. But I couldn't *not* act."

"I don't know why you had to go and be all reasonable and stuff. I was perfectly happy to be mad at you for being stupid and thoughtless and now you go and make sense and I have to agree."

He'd never scrub the memory of how she looked there, just as she collapsed, from his brain. The terror still stank on his skin. He'd wanted to kill Lex and Jack for letting her get into danger. Had blamed himself. Blamed Ben for calling her out to Chicago. But in the end, she was right. She did what an Alpha did and she did it well.

People that had snubbed her just a few days prior had sent flowers and made phone calls to check in on her health. Of course she hadn't thought of publicity when she did it, but it sure as hell had been a fabulous bump in how the rest of Cascadia perceived her.

Lex tapped on the door just a bit later and entered with Jack, whose hair was still wet from a shower.

He fell to his knees before her, hanging his head. "I failed you."

Grace leaned down and kissed his hair, drawing him back into a sitting position. "You didn't. You did your job admirably. You took out the threat effectively and you saved lives. I was getting out of that car to help Megan. I would have done the same to help any of our wolves out there in need. I didn't ask you in here to yell at you." She looked up and Jack and smiled at him too. "Or you. Sit down."

"What's up then, shortstuff? God." He went to her and hugged her, breathing in her scent. "I'm so glad you're okay."

Cade didn't feel jealousy, a reaction he found interesting.

He understood Jack's need to touch her and be sure she was all right. He'd have felt the same way about Nina, especially before he mated with Grace.

"I am too," she said as Jack moved just a few inches away and sat. "I called you both in here to see how the investigation into who tipped Pellini Group wolves off to our location was going."

Lex looked to Cade and raised an eyebrow. Admiration raged through Cade at how perceptive she was. She'd nearly died and still hadn't missed a thing.

"We don't know. Perhaps a cell phone call was traced when you left Chicago. The only people who knew were me and Cade and the people on that plane. I know sure as hell it wasn't me or Cade and I can't see why any of you would want to get shot at."

"Did you check all our cell phones? I didn't call Cade when we took off. Tegan called when we were in the car on the way. No, wait, she called the pilot to tell him to ready the jet. Who called here?" Grace sat forward and the hair on Cade's arms rose.

"I just got a text message. I thought it was from you."

"I can't even upload photos from my cellphone! I don't know how to use the text messaging thing."

"You can stitch up a knife wound and you don't know how to text?" Cade was amused.

"Yes, well one of them is useful. You tell me which you'd rather have in a pinch." The look on her face made him want to smile but he decided it would be wise not to appear to patronize her.

Lex leaned out and told Dave to bring Cade's BlackBerry.

"It had the correct info. The time you'd be arriving. Little x's and o's, you know love and hugs."

She wrinkled her nose. "And you thought that was from me?"

"Well sure! Is it too much to believe you'd send love?"

She snorted. "No. But really, do I seem the x and o type to you?"

"The pilot? Did we check him?" Jack asked.

"Yes. The same guy who's been flying our Pack around for fifteen years. He's clean." Lex opened up Cade's BlackBerry and looked at it, scanning the message.

"The company? You go through a company for this pilot?"

Lex looked at Jack and stood. "Shit. Let's go." He didn't wait for Cade's permission, he knew what had to be done and Cade knew his brother enough to know he'd do it. If anyone had betrayed them, they needed to be questioned and then dealt with. His mate was nearly killed, as was his sister. There was no forgiveness for such behavior.

"Go on and get to your meeting." Grace didn't speak of what Lex might be off doing. "I'm going to sleep for another few hours and then I'm going to the lab."

He sighed, seeking patience from the universe. "Fine. Sleep at least four more hours. Eat another full meal and I'll accompany you to the lab and let you stay for two hours. This isn't negotiable and yes, I'm being heavy-handed. I love you, I get to be."

Rolling off the bed, he held the blankets back for her to slide under and he tucked her in. "I'm glad you're here with me. I don't think I could survive without you."

Her serious brown eyes looked up into his. "We can survive all sorts of things."

"I wouldn't want to."

Her beautiful lips turned up into a smile. “Oh, well, okay then. I’m glad I’m here with you too.”

Chapter Thirteen

Grace woke up and took a shower, working out the soreness in her muscles. After dressing and dealing with minimal hair and make-up, she headed out and saw Dave just outside the door to her room.

"Hey there. You okay?"

He got to his knees. "You could have died and it would have been my fault."

She sighed. No one did guilt better than male wolves. It was stunning really, their God complex made doctors look tame by comparison.

"Dave, stand up. This is silly. Don't take so much on. You're not Superman and you can't dodge bullets. I don't hold you responsible for anything but doing your best to guard me and you did, so stop. I'm going to get a cup of coffee, you can come with me." She ran a hand over his jawline before moving down the hallway, him on her heels.

Nina grinned as Grace entered the kitchen. "Hey there, teeny. How are you feeling?"

"In dire need of caffeine. Any coffee?"

"I'm making some now. Well, for Lex and the council folks in the other room. This pushy doctor told me no caffeine for the next nearly six months." One of Nina's eyebrows rose and Grace laughed.

"You have high blood pressure, Nina. The caffeine will only make it worse and then you risk having to go on bed rest for the whole pregnancy. And while seven months isn't nine months, it's still a long time to sit in bed. Chances are after you have the baby, you'll be back to normal." She poured herself a cup. "In the meantime, you can have decaf. The caffeine is very minimal."

"I'm glad you're okay." Nina ran a hand over her stomach as she spoke. Grace realized the subtle change in the woman she'd only known a few weeks. The standoffishness Nina had shown had disappeared and she treated Grace with the same snarky love that she did everyone else. That sort of acceptance made her feel a lot more comfortable living in the house.

"Me too. Listen, I'll schedule your prenatal exams this week and get the info your way. I've been thinking of putting a small health clinic down where the lab is. The equipment is there and I don't know why we shouldn't use it. I can see you here most of the time but occasionally, you'll want to come down there so we can do an ultrasound and that sort of thing."

"Oh an ultrasound? I can see the baby and know the sex and stuff?"

"If you like, I can try and determine the gender. No guarantees the baby will cooperate. Sometimes they just turn and show you their little butts instead of whatever they're packing—or not, as it were. You hungry?" Grace grabbed a bagel and popped it in the toaster as she rummaged through the fridge.

"No, I just ate. Lex shows up every hour to shove food at me. He's already a good dad. I just hope I can be a good mom."

Grace put the food on the counter and took Nina's hands.

"You will be."

"I didn't have a very good example."

The mantle of being an Alpha was heavy. She wondered how Cade handled it, feeling the emotions of all his wolves this way for so long. Nina's worry sat on her tongue like bitter fruit.

"I don't know the whole story. Just what you've shared. But I know you gave your all to your brother, even when you were just a kid and despite his bad choices, he still came to you when he was in trouble. He knew you'd be there for him. And in the end, what I hear about him was that he'd become a decent member of the Pack. A good man." She shrugged. "Seems to me, a kid growing up on the streets the way he did along with you, that's down to you. The good man part. It's going to be all right. You'll learn, Lex will learn and the kid will own you." Grace grinned. "Anyway, Beth will be over here every day and you can always call Layla."

"What about you?"

"Me? My parents gave birth to two children and only one was ever important to them. I don't think I had much of an example either."

"You're a doctor. You're compassionate and giving. I think you'll be a great mother when the time comes. And Cade will dote and dote because that's his way." Nina snorted and Grace piled stuff on her bagel.

"You have something to tell me, honey?" Cade said as he strolled into the room.

"Hmpf. That was a hypothetical discussion." Although they hadn't taken a bit of precaution against pregnancy, it wasn't that easy for wolves to get pregnant anyway. "It's time to go to the lab. Did the samples arrive yet?"

He put his arms around her and hugged her, kissing the side of her face and neck. She didn't even pretend to be annoyed, it felt so good.

"You smell good. And yes, they did and I sent them straight over but eat that first. Everyone knows not to touch a thing until you arrive."

"You want anything?"

"No I'm good. I ate after you went back to sleep and I've eaten my weight in cookies." He paused and she grinned. "Yes, I baked earlier. You know, some men get lap dances when they're stressed. You should be grateful I bake."

She turned in his arms and looked up at him. "I *love* that you bake cookies when you're stressed. And some men don't have wives who'd tear their throats out if they ever let another female grind their feminine parts over their husband's wedding tackle. You do."

He leaned down and nipped her bottom lip. "You know it makes me hot when you're violent, right?"

"You can collect your carnal due later on tonight. I have work to do." Getting up on her tip-toes, she kissed him quickly and turned back to her sandwich.

Cade sat back and watched her dive in to her work at the lab. He also didn't fail to miss the way the wolves showed her even more deference and respect. News of what she'd done to save Megan had spread quickly. People saw it in two ways. First as a commentary of what Pellini was capable of but secondly, proof their new Alpha was worthy of her position.

No doubt he was relieved. It hurt him to see anyone in the Pack snub her. He knew she felt it, even if she'd protested that she understood it. And in a selfish way, it made him feel better to know the wolves in Cascadia understood the worth of his mate.

She moved through the lab, wearing a white coat and carrying a notebook. Occasionally, she'd stop at a microscope or a computer terminal for a bit. He made phone calls but never let her out of his sight. Nearly losing her was too raw to get past at that stage.

She didn't waste a single movement. He'd realized over the time she'd been in his life how economical everything about her was. She didn't waste words or movement. If she said it, it *needed* to be said and it came from her heart. He liked that precision about her, found it sexy. Well, he found everything about her sexy excluding that whole nearly dying thing.

After two hours had passed he waited for her to notice him. But she was focused, her face a mask of concentration as she sat at a computer terminal.

"Grace?" He approached quietly, working as hard as he could not to touch her even though he wanted to.

"Hmm?" she answered absently without even looking up.

"Two hours is up. About twenty minutes ago."

Dragging her eyes from her screen, she turned to him and took his measure. He didn't want to stop her work, he knew it was important but damn it, she'd nearly died just the day before!

He lowered his voice and pulled up a chair. "I know you're busy and this is all very important, but you promised. You need to rest."

"I'm only just hours away from a few answers. I'm not a virologist and I've had to re-learn a lot of stuff but this data from Warren's lab is huge."

"Grace, I respect that. I do. After a good night's sleep you'll be even more able to concentrate and chase those answers." Giving in to his desire, he brushed the pad of his thumb over her bottom lip.

"That's not fair."

"What isn't?" He held back a smile, barely. If he had to use sex to get her in line, he would. When it came to her well-being he wasn't above doing whatever he had to do.

"I'm going to get even with you."

He laughed, satisfied when she turned and began to turn off her computer. "I can't wait."

Grace leaned into Cade as he opened her car door and she slid in after kissing his shoulder. As much as she liked the Wardens and being so accepted by their large warm embrace, she wouldn't have complained if her living room wasn't always full of people and noise.

Still, all the people filled her up, made the Alpha wolf inside her calm and gentle against the agitation of finding a vaccine, of the frustration of not being able to protect her people as fully as she wanted right when she wanted.

But living with all those people underfoot curbed her ability to just be with Cade. To be Cade and Grace rather than the Alpha couple or relatives or whatever. It got tiring to be on all the time.

"Cade?"

He turned to her, his face lit by the yellow glow of the exterior lights of the secured lot. "Yes?"

"Can we go to dinner?"

"Are you hungry? I'm sure there's a full fridge at home. I'll make you something when we get back. I'm sorry I didn't even think about that."

Dave looked at her in the rearview, she realized *he* understood what she meant.

"Yes, yes I'm hungry but well..." She paused seeking the

right words. "I just want some time alone with you." Couple time where she didn't have to share him with a dozen other people.

He was quiet and she waved it away. "Never mind. Dave, let's go home."

Cade touched her face as Dave pulled away from the lot. "Are you unhappy at the house?"

"No. No it's not like that. I...it's just that I have to share you all the time. I realize it's who you are, who *we* are but I realized earlier we don't have much time just you and me."

"I'm sorry you're not happy. It's just this war and I have so much to deal with."

"I didn't say I was unhappy. I'm not. I'm happy." She shook her head. "Never mind. Really. I'm fine. I'm sure you're right and after this we'll have time."

He looked at his watch and she stiffened. She didn't want dinner out to be yet another thing he had to shove into his schedule. He was under enough pressure.

"Another time. I'm tired actually."

"Honey, how can I make you happy?"

She smiled and hoped it reached her eyes. "I am. I said that already a few times. Let's just go home and I'll get dinner there."

He looked as if he struggled for words and then simply put an arm around her shoulders, sitting back next to her.

Once back at the house, she wasn't surprised to stumble upon over a dozen people in their living room. While Gabe, Tracy and Nick had left for Portland earlier in the afternoon, it seemed the rest of her extended family was visiting.

Jack sprawled on a club chair and grinned as they came into the room. "Hey there, shortstuff and her mate."

"Hello, Jack." Cade pulled her closer and she resisted the

urge to roll her eyes.

"Hey, handsome. I figured you'd gone back to Boston, this is a pleasant surprise." She grinned. She did like the look of him there all ridiculously handsome and dangerous at the same time. "How long can we hog you for?" She moved to him and kissed his cheek.

"I need to get back tomorrow first thing. I wanted to help Lex with a little problem we discussed earlier. It's taken care of now so I need to get home to relay some information to Templeton." His blue eyes flashed. They must have found something wrong with the company that sent out pilots for the plane.

"Ah. Okay. Why don't you and Lex join me in my office for a few minutes." Cade turned to her. "I'll be with you in an hour or so. Be sure to eat, Grace." He cocked his head and she rolled her eyes for real.

"Go on. I'll see you in a bit."

"I was thinking about making dinner. Shall we toss something together?" Megan stood from where she'd been surreptitiously staring at Jack.

"Good idea."

They started preparation, Grace tossing some chicken and steak onto the indoor grill while Megan and Nina worked on side dishes.

"He's very handsome. But Boston is a very long way away." Grace looked at Megan as she sliced onions.

"He's smoking hot, that's what he is. Good God. I have to ask, naked?"

Surprised, Grace laughed. "Well, um, I didn't see all of him. Just certain parts. Those parts were more than adequate. He says he doesn't have a girlfriend right now."

"I'd nail him. If I was single and not knocked up and stuff." Nina shrugged with a grin.

"He's only got eyes for Grace right now." Grace looked up, alarmed, but Megan shook her head. "No, don't worry. It's natural. You just did the tri-bond with him a few weeks ago. In a while it'll ease up for him maybe. And if I'm still horny and hot and we're in the same state at the same time, I'll jump him then."

"But you'd rather find your mate?" Grace turned the meat.

"Sure. I'm getting older, I want that connection you all have. At this point, dating seems pointless."

Later, after dinner, after Grace had said her good nights and retired to the solitude of their bedroom, she thought about what Megan had said. A biological gift in many ways, the older a werewolf got, the harder it was to live without a mate. She'd been so consumed by her job and then dealing with Warren she hadn't really *had* a romantic life. For wolves like Dave and Megan fully immersed in Pack life surrounded by mated couples, it had to be much more difficult.

She read in bed for a while, not wanting to sleep until Cade finished up. His hour had long since passed but she understood all this stuff was complicated and took time. Still, she realized how much of her life he'd filled up when she missed his presence so acutely.

Cade quietly entered the room and saw her sleeping, a book open on her lap. His hour had turned into four as they'd discussed the traitor who'd sold information about their whereabouts to Warren Pellini. That information had nearly killed his wife and sister.

Lex and Jack had gotten their information and the man was no longer a threat. He was no longer anything. The pilot checked out, lucky for him, but they'd no longer use a service and Lex would do all the piloting for Cascadia higher-ranked wolves until the war was over. Jack would go back on a plane Templeton was sending out and the other Packs had been notified of this issue and were instituting their own safety measures.

She'd been upset earlier. He knew the smile she'd given him wasn't real but he had too much on his mind and he knew she understood that too.

Standing there, looking at her in his very large and formerly empty bed, she put things in perspective. His impatience at this war was more personal. Warren Pellini's bullshit stopped him from being able to have alone time with his woman. She spent her days in the lab and he in one meeting after another, one call after the other.

With a quiet sigh, he turned off the lights and headed to the bathroom to take a shower before joining her in bed.

But she apparently had other ideas when she stepped into the enclosure with him about five minutes later.

"Look, I've got the big bad Alpha all alone and helpless," she murmured before kissing his chest just over his heart.

"Should I fear for my virtue?"

She laughed and took the soap from his hands. "Let me get your back."

Dutifully, he turned and closed his eyes as she touched him. He choked on a gasp when her hands moved around to his belly and then she grabbed his cock.

"You should really be resting. You're a test on my self-control. Wet, gorgeous and so damned sexy I can barely breathe."

"Why self-control? Am I asking for that?"

He turned and backed her against the wall. “You were gravely injured just a day ago. Sex is the last thing you need, Grace.”

“Sex is exactly what I need. I need you inside me, filling me up and making the fear go away.”

He frowned at her. “Why are you afraid? God, honey, you know I’d die to protect you. I know I didn’t and you almost died.” He shoved a hand through his hair and stepped out of the shower, turning off the water and drying off.

She stood there, trembling but not leaving the enclosure.

“Let me dry you off. Let me do something for you.”

“Am I just so bad at this whole thing?” Her voice was so small, it tore at him and he picked her up and began to dry her himself but the trembling didn’t stop.

“Bad at what? Are you all right? You’re shaking and really beginning to worry me.”

“This!” She angrily waved her hand between them.

“What are you talking about?” He turned and found a pajama shirt. Once he’d pulled it over her head, he ushered her into the room and yanked the blankets back. “Get in there before you turn blue.”

“I’m not cold!” She actually stomped her foot and he felt her through the link. Fear.

“Do you want to leave? To go somewhere safer where you’re protected better? Don’t you think I don’t obsess about what happened yesterday a million times a day?”

“Are you trying to get rid of me?”

“Why do I feel like you and I are on a hidden cell phone talking to other people having totally different conversations? Tell me what’s wrong so I can fix it. If you hate me, if I make you unhappy, just tell me.” He fell to his knees.

"You're the one who can't bear to be alone with me for three minutes. You say you'll be back in an hour and it's four. You tiptoe through our bedroom and take a shower but when I show up you can't get out fast enough."

"That's bullshit! And unfair. I'm trying to keep my people alive, I'm sorry if I can't be with you every minute of the day. I truly am because I'd love to be and I'm not being sarcastic. I'm trying to take care of you and a million other people all at once. It's a lot to have on your shoulders."

"Well I do apologize for being a burden on you. God knows I'm quite aware I'm yet another thing on your to do list. I can't be all bitchy like Nina or a warrior like Tegan. I'm sure I'm a disappointment to you. Do you imagine Nina's face when you fuck me?"

He froze, her pain sliced through his anger. His anguish. Their exhaustion and worry for the other. Her fear was *for* him, not of him or for herself.

He surged up and pushed her back to the bed. One-handed he ripped the front of the pajama top open and exposed her skin to his. "That's beneath you. And you know it." He kissed a hot line down the tendon at the side of her neck and she arched into him, pulling him closer with legs she wrapped around his waist. "You're all I think of. If you're safe. If you're happy. If you're well. I just want you. Always you. Only you."

"Then for heaven's sake fuck me."

On a strangled laugh, he guided his cock to her gate, groaning when he found her hot and slick-wet. One flex of his hips and he was inside. She writhed against him, cunt tightening around his cock as she made soft, needy sounds.

"You're not a burden to me. You complete me, damn you." He rolled, bringing her atop him.

She planted her hands on his ribs and rose and fell over

him. "Then stop acting like it. I'm not going to break. I'm your partner not your ward. When I grab your package in the shower it's not for pity, it's because I want you. If I was too weak for sex, I wouldn't be riding you like a pony right now, would I?" She paused, panting as she increased her speed, grinding herself into him on her downstrokes. "And if you blame yourself for what happened yesterday once more I'm going to twist your balls right off."

He winced. "You're a mean little thing. And good lord your pussy is tight. You're my woman to protect. Of course I—um, worry about what happened yesterday. Don't blame myself of course!" he added quickly and she laughed.

"Werewolf males have an annoying tendency to think they can control everything in the world when they can't. Warren has money, he used it to betray me, betray you, betray his people. That's who *he* is. This subject is making me squicky so stop it now and make with the sexin'."

"Always. But one last thing, you're not a disappointment to me. Not ever. I'm so amazed by you. Awed. Proud. Thankful. You're more than I ever imagined my wife would be." He ran his hands over all of her he could touch, marveling in her very presence.

"If you die, I will be so pissed off." She leaned down and captured his mouth with hers.

Sliding his hands down her back, he cupped her ass, holding her open and reaching around his cock to find her clit and circle it as he thrust up into her.

"I said I was going to wait until you'd recovered more but I can't resist you when you're being all quizzical. Now come for me," he murmured.

She gave him that squeak he loved so much and her cunt rippled around his cock as she came. What he hadn't quite expected was to feel her teeth sinking into his chest just above his nipple.

Sensation, feral and hot, rushed from the spot she held in her mouth to his cock and he exploded inside her.

Sometime later, she rolled off and into the curve of his body that'd been made just for her. "Oh. Well then. Thank you. I feel very lucky too. But I worry about you. I worry one day you won't come home. It's a dangerous time right now."

He kissed her. "I'm careful. You're careful, or you will be. And we'll make it through. When this is over, you and I are going away for a while. Just us."

"Good. I want to hog you all to myself."

"You know, and I hesitate to bring this up, but all that could have been avoided if you just said what you felt right up front. I want you to be honest with me. I was afraid you hated me," Cade said.

"I'm sorry I'm so bad at this. It's not like I've had a dozen boyfriends."

He felt, rather than saw her annoyance and it made him want to laugh. For all her precision, she was still a woman, still partly human and thus, as fallible as he was at the relationship stuff.

"You're perfect."

"Nicely said."

Chapter Fourteen

Grace awoke early and got out of bed, hoping to take advantage of the quiet and get some work done. In a rare moment, Cade still slept. As much as he'd had to deal with over the last weeks, she left him that way. He couldn't run on adrenaline forever and crashing right as he needed the energy wouldn't help anyone.

Plus, she thought as she looked down at him, tawny skin stretched taut over muscles, he looked really good. Before she jumped on him, she took one long, last look and headed out.

Of course the moment she stepped out her door, two guards were there. She sighed.

"Morning, Hiroshi, Dave. I need to get working today."

"All right, Grace. We'll escort you down. Does Cade know?"

"He's sleeping and he needs the rest. Don't you dare wake him up." She saw their anxiety. "Look, guys, he's sleeping, I like it that way. You'll both be with me. The lab is like some secret governmental facility with all that security. I'm not hiding where I'm going and I'm not being unsafe. Come on, I'll even let you take me in that ridiculous Hummer. As long as someone runs to grab me breakfast when we get to the lab."

She continued to walk until she reached the kitchen. Nina, another early riser, was up and shuffling around. Lex sat at the table and watched her with hungry eyes. It made Grace smile and she liked to think Cade looked at her that way too.

"Good morning. Want some coffee? I like to watch other people drink it while I suffer in silence." Nina snickered.

"Silence? Yeah, sure," Lex mumbled and Nina tossed a pot holder at him.

"That'd be great. In a to-go cup please, I'm on my way to the lab. And before you ask, Cade is sleeping and he should stay that way. Your brother needs the down time." Thank goodness Lex was sitting so she could attempt imperious by looking down at him instead of up into his towering face. She spoke as his Alpha and she saw it flash in his eyes but then it eased and he nodded.

"I agree. Dave, add one more guard and take the Hummer."

She wanted to grin at her victory but instead touched his arm and turned to Nina, who winked and handed her a cup.

"Coffee to go. Did you write him a note at least? Because, you know he's going to be grumpy when he wakes up and you're gone."

"I did leave him a note with my schedule on it, yes. I know he thinks he can be in a hundred places all at once, protecting everyone and everything but he can't and I have a job to do and I don't want to hinder his job with it. If he has to babysit me every time I go to the lab, how can he get his work done here?"

"You're right of course. I'm his guard for the time being, until this is finished and we can relax a bit." Lex gave her an appraising and, unless she was mistaken, appreciative look.

Twelve hours later, she reached up to rub her aching neck only to have her hands moved, replaced by big, warm, sexy hands.

She breathed deep and Cade overran any scents of the lab. She leaned back into him. "Hi there."

He kissed the top of her head. "Quitting time, Dr. Warden."

"I'm on to something here, Cade."

"You can find it the day after tomorrow. Tomorrow is the Joining ceremony and our house is already bursting with people. Dinner is in ninety minutes. My mother was going to come down here herself so you should thank me."

She turned. "Oh my gosh, I'm so sorry. I totally forgot. Let me shut this down and set up this other program to run all night." She kissed him quickly and turned back around to finish up.

He sat and she felt his warmth just behind her. It filled an empty space she hadn't realized was the source of her discomfort over the day.

"I shouldn't tell you this, it'll only make your ego bigger." She turned to him after she'd hung her lab coat up on a peg and grabbed her bag. "But I really missed you today."

He smiled, slow and sexy. The way he approached her, muscles moving against the tight, dark shirt he wore, branded him a predator and she wasn't so very unhappy to be his prey.

"Good. I missed you too. Thank you for your note and for taking along another guard. I wasn't pleased to wake up alone, but I do hear you growled at anyone who thought of waking me up. I like that, being protected by you." He pulled her close, one arm around her waist. With no more than a slight bit of energy, she found herself being dragged up that hard wall of chest and meeting his mouth with hers.

"Can I tell you a secret?" she asked, her lips against his.

"Yes. Especially if it's dirty."

"The whole big guy thing you do? All strong and stuff? It

really, really does it for me."

He laughed and she swallowed the sound greedily. "Good. Now, you don't need to feel guilty about forgetting. You've had a few more things on your mind than the Joining ceremony."

She put her arms around his neck as he walked them out. Dave kept his eyes averted but Grace did see his smile.

Cade had woken up without her there, without her warmth, her smell still on his skin. He'd seen the note she'd left on her pillow and smiled. She had things to do and he wasn't going to be able to stop her.

He'd read her precise, neat, uniform writing as she detailed her day for him and smiled. Minx. She'd closed with her wish for him to sleep as long as possible so he could rest up and her worry he wasn't getting enough down time. And after that, she'd even given him one little x and one little o. Disarming.

Still, he'd given her the space to do her job and as soon as he'd headed into the main house he'd been barraged by one thing after the other until he looked at the clock and realized it was already after five and he went to get his woman himself.

She sat, body pressed against his the whole ride home and didn't complain about the Hummer once. He knew how much she hated the giant vehicle so she must have accepted the fact that it was necessary for her safety.

"I will say my dress arrived the day before I left for Chicago."

He looked down at her. "Dress?"

"For the Joining?"

"Ah! Okay. Security is going to be insanely tight tomorrow and it won't be the full ceremony you deserve but Ben and Tegan can't be here because of the war. Apparently Tegan is pretty pissed about that. When this is over, and yeah, I'm sure you're as sick of hearing it as I am of saying it, we'll do something that befits you."

She sighed and looked up at him. "Do you really think that sort of thing matters to me? I'm already yours. This ceremony is about the Pack and your family really. So fine. But it doesn't change what already is."

Dave laughed from the front seat as they drove through the various checkpoints at the house. Cade hated living in an armed camp but with the increasing levels of violence he had little choice.

She followed him out of the car, even letting him pick her up to help get her to the ground but when she caught wind of the din coming from the house she stiffened.

"Are you still having problems with Nina? I thought you two had become fast friends." He pulled her to the side and motioned for the guards to give them some space. Lex went to the stairs leading to the house and took point, eyes scanning the horizon.

"No, everything is fine between us. I can't say I'm totally comfortable knowing the depth of her feelings for you, but now that I've got Jack as my anchor I can understand it and I know she loves Lex. Why do you ask?"

"You just got very tense."

"We can talk about it later. Let's go inside." She averted her eyes.

He stopped her, tipping her chin so he could see her face. "Honey, tell me now. Don't you remember last night?"

That sweet mouth of hers curved into a sly smile and he laughed. "Not that part, well, okay I'm glad you remember that part. The fight part."

"I just like quiet. And solitude. Not a whole lot here. I've lived on my own for many years and I just never feel alone here. I'll get used to it, I'm sure. I *like* your family. I just don't want to be with fifteen other people every moment of the day."

"Part of it is..."

"I hate to break this up but people heard the cars pulling up, some are moving this way," Lex called out.

Her spine slumped a bit and he sighed. "Thanks, Lex." Looking back down into a face he'd already fallen deeply and irrevocably in love with, he smiled. "I'm sorry. Can we talk about this later?"

"Sure. Let's go."

The smile she wore didn't light up her eyes the way he'd seen her in unguarded moments but she walked in and embraced her position without hesitation. His family responded to her, he realized. Responded to her natural sense of order and calm. Whereas the Wardens in general were raucous and loud, when she was around he noticed they tended to be more affectionate. His grandmother told him earlier that day when she'd brought their rings by, that a good Alpha match was like theirs. Two halves of a whole that complemented the other.

Chapter Fifteen

Even mid-summer in the northwest could be chilly, and the morning of the Joining ceremony, a bite hung in the air, fighting with the growing influence of growth and fecundity. Grace had sat, watching the sun rise as Tracy had wound flowers through her hair. They'd fall away when she transformed into a wolf, but until then, they'd be very pretty.

"This dress is so lovely." Megan motioned her head at Grace. "I don't know that I've ever seen anything like it."

"Thank you. It was a huge splurge. There's this vintage clothing shop, near the hospital I used to work at. I knew they got stuff like this in from time to time and I checked their website. When I saw it, I knew I had to have it. I can't believe it fits me so well."

Splurge was a minor word compared to how much she'd spent on the 1950s' era Mainbocher dress. Pale pink silk, close-fitting bodice and trailing down to her ankles. She felt like a goddess in the dress and hoped Cade saw it that way as well.

"You look like one of those Hollywood starlets from the forties." Tracy stepped back. "Perfect. You're ready to go. I'll tell everyone and we can get started. Are you all right?"

Grace nodded. "I am. I've been ready since I walked into that room and laid eyes on Cade the first time." He'd been so breathtakingly gorgeous, her hormones had done the samba.

She'd nearly jumped out of her skin when she carefully walked toward the stairwell leading to the meadow out back where everyone waited. Jack stood there wearing a tux and grinning.

"I came to walk you to Cade. That okay with you?"

Tears sprang to her eyes. "Oh! Yes, more than okay, it's wonderful. Thank you. It means so much to me."

He bent and kissed her, just a brief brush of his lips over hers. "It's my pleasure, Grace. I love you. Don't panic, we all three know our place in this little triangle. But it pleases me to make you smile that way. And I wouldn't miss this day. I have to fly back out again to do some business down south and then in a few more places to check out what our Enforcers are doing with their training. But for the next four hours or so, I'm here for you and Cade."

She took the arm he held out and they walked together.

Cade stood there, sheltered by an arch marked by intricate carvings. Wolves, she discovered as they got closer. Real wolves stood at attention all around the area, guarding her entrance into Cascadia.

Most of the ceremony went by in a blur. Grace felt as if she were underwater. Cade looked amazing there, a breeze ruffling his hair. He wore no shirt, a ceremonial nod to giving his mate the shelter of his body and his Pack.

She spoke words older than her people's presence on the continent and at some point she'd been handed a sharp blade. The slice into her flesh, the metallic scent of her blood hitting the earth and the subtle shift in the air as Cade's joined hers at their feet.

Howls on the breeze.

Her dress sliding from her skin as she stepped from it. Standing naked under the sky until she'd slipped her skin and looked at the world through wolf eyes.

And then they'd run.

Far. Far as the earth beneath her feet welcomed her, as the Pack took her in and she became Cascadia with a surety her wolf recognized and became quieted by.

As wolves, Cade took her, his teeth buried in the fur at her neck.

She reclined in the soft loam of the forest floor and watched the wolves, *her* wolves run and play, enjoy themselves. It was one of the first truly carefree moments she'd witnessed since she'd arrived in Seattle and it made her heart glad.

Cade stood on the deck, drinking a glass of wine, watching the stars. It'd been the second best day of his life, right after meeting and claiming Grace. She'd looked like a little smidge of heaven as she'd floated across the grass in that pink dress. So feminine and beautiful with flowers in her hair.

She'd loved their rings and had gifted him with such a smile, his heart had stuttered. How he'd gotten so lucky in the midst of all this turmoil he didn't know but he didn't plan to question it.

"Cade, I'm sorry to bother you, Templeton is on the phone." Megan came out onto the deck.

Grace stirred from her chair where she'd been curled up like a kitten, just watching him as he watched the sky. They'd retreated to their room earlier and had made love for hours. His muscles were relaxed, languid as he turned to her.

He gulped down the wine and held his hand out to her and she took it.

They sat in his office, he didn't want her far so he pulled her into his lap and she'd just made herself comfortable.

"Okay, what's up?" he asked, stroking an idle fingertip up and down Grace's arm.

"I've got Maxwell on the line as well as Georges from Siskiyou. Are Nick and Gabe there?"

"Yes," both men answered from across the room.

"Well I'll get right to it. Warren Pellini was in contact an hour ago. He's called A Challenge of Council."

A collective intake of breath left the air in the room electric with tension.

"Is that even legal? He's shunned. Technically he's not in any position to use the old laws against anyone," Gabe said quietly.

"We don't have to honor it. Not technically. But he's made the Challenge publicly and has agreed to call his wolves off if he loses. The war would be over," Templeton said.

"But at what cost? Why even let Warren Pellini cherry pick our laws when it suits him? He's the one who broke Palaver." Anger coursed through Cade. And some concern.

"Two humans were murdered today in Los Angeles. It's most certainly Pellini Group wolves who did it. Ripped apart and left in the foothills east of downtown. The FBI has been in contact through Agent Benoit. This is increasingly difficult to manage. They want it to end or they'll get involved. Benoit told me higher ups are discussing legislation that would register the entire werewolf population. This isn't like the old days when we could simply fight pitch battles out in open fields. Humans are everywhere and Warren is involving them to protect himself," Jack said simply.

"So you're saying you're going to do this, Templeton?"

Grace turned and stood, moving behind him and beginning to knead his shoulders.

"I've been poisoned," Templeton said simply.

Cade leaned forward, as did the other wolves in the room. "What? What?"

An uproar sounded over the conference call and it took a few long minutes to get things back under order.

"Explain please." Cade tried to let her fingers relax him but it wasn't working too well.

"This afternoon, when I was still on my way back, he took Carla to the grocery store. With only one guard." Jack snorted and Lex joined in.

"I can tell my own damned story, Jack," Templeton broke in. "I wanted to take my wife to the market, is that so wrong? Without nineteen guards. And you were right so shut up now. Anyway, when I went to grab a buggy a bunch of people were jostling around, you know how that goes and in the jumble someone cut me. I didn't think anything of it until we got inside and Carla smelled something off, something wrong. It was the poison."

"Dichilimate?" Grace asked, moving around Cade.

"Sure is, pretty lady. I take it you know about the stuff? If so, explain it please because it's all gibberish to me," Templeton said.

Grace sat on the desk. "One of the few poisons other than silver-based that can harm us, even kill in high enough doses. But if the latter was the case, Templeton wouldn't be on the phone now. Did you spend the last few hours getting a chemical flush?"

"Yes, and it was so very pleasant. I'm gonna find the fucker who did this to me and pound a nail though his skull."

Grace's mouth hinted at a smile but she held it back. Cade shook his head and snorted.

"Okay then. So moving along, Templeton is going to have some lasting after-effects like muscle loss and weakness and most likely a course of physical therapy that will last about six months. Given that he's already in his seventies, he'll most likely never achieve the same strength he had before today. I'm sorry, Templeton."

"So you get it in one, dolly. Yes, she's correct. Right now I have to use a cane to walk, my legs are fucked up. I can change but I can't hold my wolf for very long. How come I never heard of this shit before?"

"It's extremely rare and hard to acquire. The human government invented it by accident but it's harmless to them. The only stores available are synthesized and stolen from the government labs. And almost certainly come from Warren and his operation. I've only seen it once before and that was in medical school, a textbook case. There've only been five or six confirmed cases, half were fatal. I'd guess they just wanted to maim you and call your leadership into question. And really, what better time to challenge you? Warren isn't an Alpha but he's very strong physically and certainly now can defeat you. I'm sorry, I don't mean to be flip." She looked worried and Cade didn't need to fall into their link to know she was afraid.

"Smart one you're mated to, Cade. So here's my plan. Cade will take on the Challenge in my place."

Grace stood up, fury on her face. "Oh no he won't!"

Lex had jumped up as well and everyone else looked from person to person.

"What makes you think I'm the best choice, Alpha?"

Grace spun to face him, eyes narrowed, hands on her hips.

"I'm in no shape to do this. Maxwell would be another

choice but strategically, I need him to stay powerful in Chicago. We can't be weak in Pellini's backyard. And we need to keep Great Lakes powerful. They just lost an Enforcer and got a new one. The upheaval would be too much," Templeton said.

"What do you mean upheaval?" It occurred to Cade far more than this Challenge was being discussed.

"When you win, I want you to take over for me. Jack isn't an Alpha although he's very strong and he should continue to be Second here. You and Grace would be my successors. It's the natural choice, all the Nationally allied wolves would agree and you know it. You're strong. You've got the fancy letters behind your name and you hold important territory without any challenge at all. You know politics better than any wolf I've ever seen. You're the logical choice, Cade. I'm sorry this falls on your shoulders but that's where it fits best." Templeton said it and all the wolves in the room began to nod.

Except Grace, who shook her head vehemently.

"I'll fax over the proposed dates. You and I will need to discuss the transfer. I expect you'll need to speak with Lex, who is most clearly the best choice to replace you as Alpha there. Give me a call tomorrow. Carla is shooting daggers at me to go to bed, damned poison. Grace, forgive me." He hung up.

"Well, that was unexpected." Nina looked back and forth between Cade and Lex. "Grace will have some knowledge of what Pellini's physical form is like, and Tee too, I'd expect. Good thing you work out all the time."

"This isn't going to happen." Grace's voice was very quiet.

"Grace, it has to. He's right. He can't do it, Maxwell can't do it. I'm the strongest and most powerful wolf in the country after those two. I can beat Warren. I *am* an Alpha. And to be made Supreme Alpha? It's beyond an honor. Being hand-picked is immense."

"So essentially, who fucking cares what I have to say? Is that it? Just stand off to the side and shut up?" Her voice went from soft and scarily calm to loud and scarily, well scary. She was pissed off and scared as hell.

"Grace." Tracy stood up and moved to her but Grace spun and put her hand out. The power radiated off her, pouring through the space in hot, angry rush. Cade couldn't help but be impressed.

"Don't. Is it your man who's being threatened here? No. No. Not your man, not yours either." She turned to Nina. "No it's mine. And so don't try to pooh pooh it and talk to me about duty because I. Will. Not. Have. It."

"Grace, settle down." Cade moved toward her. "Honey, I know you're scared but I'm going to win. There's no question of that."

"There's no question because it's not happening."

"I don't want to fight about this but this is my duty."

"You made your choice." She turned and left the room, slamming it so hard pictures fell off the wall.

"Dave, be sure she's all right but give her some space," Cade said before sitting back down.

"Wow. Who'd have thought she had all that in her?" Tracy looked toward him, one eyebrow raised.

He exhaled hard, scrubbing hands over his face. "Lex, you'll need to take over for me so be sure we get all the procedure done correctly. Let's set up a meeting with Dad tomorrow and get Melissa here as well. You'll need to tap someone for Enforcer in your stead."

"Are you sure about this? She seems pretty opposed." Lex had a look on his face and Cade knew what his brother was feeling. Relief it wasn't his wife who'd flipped out and also understanding of what she must be feeling.

"Doesn't matter what she feels about it, Lex. I'm Alpha. Wardens have led Cascadia for generations. You're a fine choice and my choice is to step up and take the challenge given to me by my Alpha, just as you will. What should I do? Not accept because my wife is afraid for me? Let this monster kill our people and endanger us with the humans because I turned away from my responsibility? I don't want her to be unhappy but I will do this."

And he sat at his desk, booted his computer and began.

"Grace, wait up!" Dave called after her as she practically ran down the hall to their room.

Exasperated, she turned. "What?"

"Why don't we take a run? You'll feel better after a run. Come on. He's going to be busy for the next several hours. Don't sit in there and stew."

"I'm not sitting here. I'm going to the lab to work. I have work to do as well and since our special day is apparently not inviolate, I may as well go in. You have five minutes, after which I'm leaving and you will not stop me. You can go with me and bring Hiroshi, or you can hang out here. I don't care which. I'm grabbing a sweater and I'll meet you in the garage. Or not." She shrugged and walked into her room, picked up her beautiful dress and carefully placed it in the box and grabbed a sweater.

Dave had gone, most likely to tattle on her but she would leave in three minutes. She had a set of keys to one of the Mercedes and the little decoder that allowed the engine to engage too.

"Hey, Tiny, hang on a second."

Grace prayed for strength as she tossed her stuff into the

front seat of the car and turned. “Nina, just...don’t.”

“I’m sorry. I just wanted to say I’m sorry and I wish things were different.” Nina actually looked at a loss for words and for a moment Grace waited for space/time to fold in on itself.

“Well, that’s up to Cade. I’m leaving now. Go to sleep, you’re going to be facing a lot of stress over the next weeks.”

“Not, *leaving* leaving though, right?” Nina asked.

“No, not *leaving.* Just going to work. I need some space just now, to think and process. Go on.” She shooed Nina.

Dave hustled down the steps with Hiroshi and frowned until she handed him the keys.

“We’re not taking the Mercedes, Grace. Cade, or rather Lex says you take the Hummer every time you leave the property.”

“Fine.” She grabbed her stuff but Nina stopped her.

“Don’t let this get between you and Cade. He loves you but he has a duty.”

“And God knows I’m used to being second best.” She would *not* cry.

“I know what you’re feeling, Grace. You know how I was changed right? That I was attacked and challenged at a Pack dinner and the entire Pack stood by and watched as their Third tried to kill me? You don’t know how much I hated Lex and Cade both for that. Over the years I’ve come to know a lot about Cade Warden. He’s a man of intense honor and he *believes* in the rule of law that’s kept the wolves safe for centuries. I’m not making excuses for him, just explaining from another perspective. I know what you’re feeling. You’re afraid for him. Afraid he’ll die and you’ll be alone. Afraid he’s choosing responsibility over you. But he cannot do anything else and hold his head up. You know that. He loves you, Grace. Help him here.” Nina kissed her cheek and stepped back to allow her to get into the huge vehicle. Dave and Hiroshi knew better than to pick her up.

"Go, damn it. I'm your Alpha too. If you can't obey me, let me drive and leave me alone." She sounded sullen and she knew it. It wasn't something she did usually but she'd had enough. Everyone had their limits.

They left her alone the trip over to the lab and once they got inside, they made themselves comfortable in the staff lounge area while she worked. If her stupid mate was going to risk his life by fighting her worthless brother, she had to get that vaccine working beforehand.

Cade looked up at the clock and saw it was nearly three in the morning. "Go to bed, Lex. Your pregnant wife is all alone. There's not much else we can do at this point anyway. We'll take it up again when we meet tomorrow. Or rather, later today."

He stood and stretched.

"You going to be all right? Give her a break, Cade. She's afraid for you. This isn't about big Pack politics for her, this is about her mate." Lex squeezed his shoulder on the way out. "You go to bed too."

"I'm on my way there now. Thanks, Lex."

"Yeah well, thank you too, huh? For believing I have it in me to fill your shoes." Lex ducked his head a bit.

"I admire you, Lex. You're a damned good leader. No stretch to believe you'll do just fine."

"Jeez, any minute and we're gonna start weeping. I'm going to bed to show my woman some sexual prowess or something," Lex grumbled and headed toward his and Nina's room.

Cade snorted and headed to his room. He'd been thinking

of how he'd make some renovations to build some more private rooms on their side of the house to give Grace some space that was hers but if he planned to take over for Templeton, he supposed the point was moot.

Even more moot when he entered their room and she wasn't there.

He picked up the phone but her cell was on voicemail so he called Dave.

"What the hell?"

"She's working, Cade. Just leave it alone right now," Dave said without preamble.

"It's three in the damned morning. She needs to be here. Bring her ass home or I'll come and get her."

"You're awfully good at making all her choices these days, aren't you? If you come down here, you'd better watch your balls because she's in a sour mood." Dave hung up.

"Did he just hang up on me?" Cade sighed and began to pace. He opened their link but aside from a general level of agitation, didn't get a whole lot more than that. She had either cut him off, which was very difficult, or she was deeply involved in whatever she was doing. Knowing Grace, he'd lay odds on the latter.

He tossed his clothes in the hamper and climbed in bed but instead of sleeping, he tossed and turned for an hour before getting back up and grabbing the phone again.

"What?" Dave answered.

"You're awfully lippy to your Alpha," Cade drawled.

"I'm trying to sleep on a very small break room couch, I'm not in a great mood. This is all your fault anyway. What do you want? She's fine. I made her take a break and eat something and she's working. I can see her from where I'm laying. Hiroshi is on watch and the place is locked up tight."

"You being there at four a.m. is my fault, how?"

Dave exhaled sharply. "I've known you my whole life. You're my cousin and my Alpha." He paused. "But you've always been the boss. Even when you were a kid. Grace gets that. She understands duty to her people. She betrayed her damned family for it. And all you had to do was take her out of the room and ask her her opinion. But you decided to risk your life, give up your position here and move to Boston to take on Supreme Alpha status and you didn't bother to pretend to value her opinion. Ah, I see by your stupefied silence you finally got that."

"Well, she could have stayed here to talk to me instead of running off down there to hide." God, he sounded like a punk.

"You're an ass. She's doing her duty just like you're doing yours. She wants that vaccine because she wants you protected for the Challenge. Now, I'm going to try and sleep some more. Hiroshi and I trade in another hour and I was up before dawn for the Joining. Remember that?" Dave hung up again.

"Crap."

Chapter Sixteen

"Grace, why don't you go home for a while?" Dave said as he approached.

She looked up and noticed the lab had filled with people. It was nearly two in the afternoon and she hadn't slept in well over twenty-four hours. Nothing new, she'd gone days without sleeping before, part of the doctor gig.

"Send Hiroshi home for a change of clothes please? I'm going to shower here and then I'll catch a few hours' sleep." They had dormitory-style rooms just for that sort of thing in the lab.

"I don't know, Grace. Cade called twice this morning. He's going to want to see you."

"Dave, I'm in the middle of something. He's busy, so am I. I'm not interrupting my work to make him feel better. Plus? I'm not so enamored of him just now." Grace told her staff she was taking a few hours to sleep and headed to one of the quiet rooms to do just that.

Her dreams were fitful, filled with images of Cade getting killed during the Challenge, damn him. But when she woke up, she knew what she'd been missing with the vaccine. Foregoing the shower, she put her lab coat back on and rushed out, shouting orders as she went.

Her staff went scurrying and began to apply the solution she'd hit on when she'd just woken up.

They worked on it for the next several hours until she knew she'd had enough. She needed a shower, a hot meal and some sleep and she supposed it was time to confront her stubborn mate as well.

"Okay." She rubbed her eyes. "Let's go home. You guys need some time off and this all has to sit for a while."

"Grace, you're a machine." Dave kissed her cheek.

"Thank you. Goodness, it's already nine-thirty? Yikes." She grabbed her bag and they headed for the door.

Outside, the air was cool but not cold and she took in the fresh, non-lab scents. But on her last deep breath as they cleared the trees and started into the lot, something not right filtered into her system. She froze just as Dave put his hand out. Hiroshi yanked her to the ground as a bullet whizzed into the place she'd just been standing.

Instead it hit the tree just behind them, and a freaking branch snapped off, hitting Dave in the head and knocking him out.

"You've got to be kidding me!"

"Stay down, Grace. I'm going to have to find him and take him out," Hiroshi whispered in her ear.

She nodded slightly, keeping herself plastered to the ground.

Hiroshi moved off like a shadow but some moments that felt like hours later, she heard the crack of the gun again and then a growl in the distance. Cade was there!

When the gun went off again she'd had it with the whole situation. She was tired and pissed off.

Cade was in the treeline, looking for a way to get to the shooter. Lex was off to his right and he reached out through the link and knew Grace was alive and unharmed. Suddenly, the bubbling heat of her rage flooded the link and he saw her moving toward the shooter so fast he couldn't believe his eyes.

He couldn't yell at her to stop or he'd put her in more danger but as he and Lex moved to get the shooter's attention, he planned to spank that pretty little ass of hers when this was all over.

Ducking and running, charging at the shooter, he watched in total amazement as his tiny wife hauled her laptop bag up and knocked the shit out of the shooter when she hit him in the head with it.

He crumpled to the ground and as Cade reached her, he heard her say, "Softball from middle school all through college."

She kicked the weapon away and turned to see him coming. Without missing a beat, she raced to him and jumped into his arms.

"Honey, what were you doing?" he asked between patting her all over to be sure she was unharmed.

"My job. Where's Hiroshi? I need my medical bag to check Dave out."

"You charged a man with a rifle, Grace. Are you out of your mind?"

She scrambled down and narrowed her eyes as she looked up at him. "Do you really want to remind me how pissed off I am at you? I still have my laptop bag. And where's Hiroshi?"

"Here! I've been hit in the shoulder."

She spun as she yelled back to them to get her bag pronto.

Lex actually had the balls to chuckle as he jogged to get her bag from inside the Hummer once their prisoner had been restrained.

She didn't say another word to him until they got back home. She ordered Dave into bed. He didn't have a concussion, just a big goose egg and once he'd transformed back at the lab, even that started to go down. Hiroshi had a bandage on his shoulder but he too managed to transform to work the silver through him. Efficiently, Grace gave people tasks and put Hiroshi to bed as well.

Lex disappeared with the prisoner and Cade didn't ask a thing. Lex had a job to do. Three other guards went with him.

"I'm starved and then I need a shower and some sleep," she announced as she walked past him and into the kitchen.

"Sit down. I'll get you something." Cade plopped her into a chair and turned to work.

"Did you just pick me up like I was furniture?"

"Are you *trying* to pick a fight? I'm making you a meal. That's a nice thing. I'd think most women would like that."

She cocked her head and a trickle of fear ran through him.

"I'm aware that because of my general nature, most people think I'm easy. And I usually am. I let most stuff roll off because in the big scheme of things, they're not important. There are a number of things I believe, Cade Warden. First, duty is important. I have a duty to serve my wolves and so, while your method of making decisions is totally selfish, sucks and treats me as if I don't matter at all, I accept your choice to do this Challenge." She slammed a hand on the table when he opened his mouth to interrupt and he closed his lips.

"However, that does not mean I'm not hurt by your seeming inability to at least *ask* me if I want to rip up my roots, once again, and become the Supreme Alpha of the United States and move to Boston. That does not mean you can just make decisions that affect us as a couple assuming I'll be fine because hey, she's easy and never complains anyway!"

Her voice rose and he moved back until the counter dug into his back. She remained seated, watching him through narrowed eyes.

"Just because I'm short doesn't mean you can pick me up like I'm a chair or something. Just because I don't flip out and start fights all the time doesn't mean you can make choices that endanger *your life* and uproot mine without even asking me! I think *most women* expect their spouses to you know, consult them on the big stuff. I don't care how you want to wear your hair, I don't care what kind of car you drive. But when it comes to oh, say challenges to the death with homicidal maniacs and essentially drafting me to become the First Lady of the werewolves, I'd like the damned courtesy of at least you pretending my voice matters!" Her eyes flashed so much hurt and fury it nearly made him lose his knees.

Instead, he went to her and knelt, putting his head in her lap. She ran her fingers through his hair with a sigh. "I love you, Cade. I'm proud of your sense of justice and duty. I really don't want you to fight Warren to the death and I'm pretty steamed at Templeton for not asking you in private. There's a lot I'm steamed about, including being shot at, yet again. But this is a relationship and I can't be happy if you make my choices for me, or make choices for us without even consulting me."

"When you ran off, I didn't get much of a chance to. But okay, before you maim me like you did that wolf at the lab, I should have spoken to you. Your opinion does matter. I'm just used to making my own choices and not having to ask. And I did not treat you like furniture. I'd have picked up Nina that way too." She growled and he quickly added, "Or Megan or anyone else. I just wanted you to sit so I could take care of you."

"I like it when you take care of me, Cade. I don't like it when you treat me like I don't matter. *Ask* me to sit. *Ask* my opinion about things. Do I want you to risk your life? No. My first reaction was to tell Templeton to suck an egg. But I'd have worked past it, I *have* worked past it. Now, I'm sorry to have scared you but that guy in the parking lot was the last damned straw, I tell you."

He sat up, amused, and kissed her. "They always say it's the quiet ones and who do I know who's quiet? But I can honestly agree with the statement now. When you work up a good mad, you really go to town. You clocked the hell out of that Pellini wolf."

"He'd better be telling us something good or I may have to find a baseball bat to show him what I meant about softball."

"My goodness, so vicious. It's very sexy when it's not directed at me." He kissed her again and once more just because he could. "You taste tired, but good. I don't like it when you're not here."

"Make me some food and I'll tell you what I've been up to in the lab."

Grace watched him, took in that spectacular behind as he made her dinner. Being waited on by a man as delicious as hers was quite a treat.

"So, not that I mind the back up or anything but why did you show up at the lab anyway? And by the way, your bottom is very nice."

He looked over his shoulder and grinned before getting back to cooking.

"You'd been at the lab for an entire day. I called and called and Dave kept telling me to leave you alone but I got sick of it and Tracy and Nina, backed up by Megan, all told me I was dumb and needed to go and see you. So I did. We got there and something wasn't right so Lex and I scouted and that's when we heard the first shot. You nearly gave me a heart attack when you broke cover and charged the gunman. Don't do that again, Grace."

"He made me mad. I'm sick of being shot at. Anyway, I'm close to a breakthrough on the vaccine. It's easier for wolves to test this sort of thing than humans because we have heartier immune systems. I'll start this week on the first pieces. Then eventually, we'll have to deal with it directly against the virus strain we took from Warren."

"How will you do that? Volunteers?"

"Yes. Two of my staff have offered. I don't want to risk it until I've done some more work. So are you going to tell me when you're scampering off to fight my brother in some sort of cage match?"

"I don't scamper, Grace, my love. I stalk like the scary wolf I am. You could at least pretend to find me fearsome." He turned and brought her a plate.

"The most fearsome omelet maker ever. And of course you're fearsome. I'm not scared of you, but I can see how others would be." She took a huge bite and felt better immediately.

"That piece was the size of your head. Take your time. I'll make you more if you're still hungry." He snickered.

"You should get started then." She indicated the stove and he laughed, leaning over to kiss her.

"After this, we're going to have sex. Lots of it."

"Okay. Let me get some orange juice then." She got up to pour them both a glass.

After she'd demolished two omelets, six slices of bacon,

toast and two peaches she finally pushed her plate away with a satisfied sigh.

"Better?"

"Much. I didn't realize how hungry I was, I guess. I did eat while at the lab, by the way, so don't lecture me. I'm not in the mood."

He hid a smile. Why he liked this prickly side of her he wasn't sure but he did. "You feeling up to sex?"

"If you do all the work, I'm up to looking at you while you're naked and making me feel good. After I shower that is."

"Go on. I need to check in with Lex. I promise it will be less than half an hour or I'll let you know."

When she got up, he couldn't help it, he grabbed her to him and kissed her for all he was worth. She softened and opened her mouth, letting him in, winding her arms around his neck as she scrambled up his body and wrapped her legs around his waist.

"Never mind. Lex can wait," he said into her mouth.

"Here. Hard. Now."

Her hands yanked at her pants as she made frustrated noises.

"Here?"

"The table is right behind me."

It sure was. He laid her down on it and she made quick work of her jeans and panties, leaving them on one leg. She glistened there, wet and ready.

"Fuck. Fuck. Hang on."

She slapped his fumbling hands out of the way and yanked them open, freeing his cock and pulled him down by the front of his shirt.

As he found her mouth for a kiss, his cock nudged the hot, wet gate of her cunt and surged into her body.

Her hum of satisfaction wrapped around his balls as he thrust. She tightened her calves around his waist and pounded his ass with her heels. In all the times they'd been together, she'd never been so wild for it. It made him wild in turn.

The scent of her skin rose as she heated for him, the scent of her honey teased the air as it invited him deeper into her pussy.

"More." Her nails dug into his shoulders. He grabbed her hips and angled her, now mindless in his need to fuck her hard, to take her, mark her, claim her again after their recent argument.

"I don't want to hurt you," he stuttered as she flexed her hips to meet his strokes.

"I'm a werewolf. Fuck me, please."

He laughed and picked up the pace. She arched in response, her body growing even more slick.

Thunk. Thunk. Thunk. The table hit the wall as he fucked into her body. He never took his gaze from her face so he caught the look of surprised pleasure when her orgasm hit, felt her cunt tighten around him.

"I love you, Cade."

Christ. That was all it took after feeling her come around him and after four more thrusts he came so hard he saw points of light in his vision.

He kissed her forehead. Then each one of her hands as he helped her up and back into her clothes.

"Now you can go talk to Lex and I'm going to shower. Meet you in our room shortly. If you're not back within half an hour, I'm hunting you down." With one last kiss, she was gone and he was left with her scent all over him and a smile on his face.

Grace took a hot shower and changed into some sweats and went to check on Dave and Hiroshi. It didn't surprise her to see Beth there pampering Dave. Dave's mother was her sister and from what Grace understood, Dave had been like another child to Beth and Henri when his mother had died.

Beth smiled at her, hugging her tight. "I'm glad to see you back. I hear there was trouble?"

"It's okay now. Honestly." She blushed, thinking of how embarrassed she'd be if her mother-in-law had wandered into the kitchen for a snack just a few minutes before.

"I can't imagine what it's going to be like for you. Not just with the Challenge but then well, being the Supreme Alpha. I'm going to miss you both so much. Just a few years ago all my children were right here and now three of them are going to live in other states. I suppose it means we'll have to visit Boston more often. I have enjoyed getting to know you, Grace."

Her mother-in-law was a very warm woman and Grace would miss her.

"One thing at a time. Let's just get through the Challenge and then we'll deal with moving. I just want that part over with."

She took Dave's vitals and checked in on Hiroshi before heading back to their room. Seeing Cade wasn't back yet, she shucked out of her sweats and into, well nothing but some lotion.

Stretching, she reveled in the slight soreness of her muscles. She'd needed to be with him like that, with him letting go of his control and taking her with such ferocity.

When he came into the room a short time later his face was

grim although it did lighten some when he saw her naked there in bed.

"Tell me."

"Your parents, Grace. They helped this assassin, not a very good one, thank God, triangulate you with your cell phone. I can't believe both Lex and I didn't even think about how your old cell would be dangerous and have it replaced."

"My parents?" She got to her knees, feeling sick. "My parents helped someone try to kill me?" She shouldn't have been so hurt, they'd rejected her when she opted to not join Warren's group and even when she'd been back in touch, she supposed in her own way she'd rejected them too.

"I'm sorry." He sighed and shook his head, holding her without saying anything else.

Sometime later, he made love to her slow and gentle. Neither of them spoke but through their hands and mouth on the other. He was her family, the one that mattered.

Chapter Seventeen

"Cade's on the phone, Grace," Dave called to her across the lab. She'd started some limited trials on the vaccine and had been putting in long hours over the week following the discovery that her parents had tried to harm her.

She picked up. "Hi there, what's up?"

"I just wanted to tell you the Challenge has been set for two weeks from tomorrow in Boston."

She suddenly had trouble finding enough air to breathe. She sat and Dave was there, his hand on her shoulder.

"Okay. I need to get working then. This has to be finished."

"I want to see you now. I'm going to have Dave drive you to me and you and I are going to sneak off for a night. We can't afford more than one, too much is going on. But you and I need the time."

"Yes. Yes. I want that too." She handed the phone to Dave who said, "uh huh" a few times and hung up. "Give me five minutes."

She dashed off and gave some instructions before grabbing her stuff and heading out. They'd doubled the guards on the lab just in case anyone else knew the location, so plenty of well-armed werewolves nodded at them as they passed before loading into the Hummer.

Dave did all sorts of switchbacks and funky driving before dropping her off at a corner where Cade waited in another SUV.

"I've got it from here. See you tomorrow." Cade nodded to Dave and helped Grace into the car.

"I have you totally all to myself? As in alone? You and me alone?"

"Yep. I packed you a bag of clothes to wear to the lab tomorrow. You won't need anything once we get where we're going."

"I like the sound of that."

Some minutes later, he pulled up to a gorgeous A-Frame style home nestled in the mountains. "Believe it or not, my parents own this. It's a vacation home. There are guards everywhere but no one will bother us."

He pulled into the garage and once the door had closed she sat back and closed her eyes. "Do you hear that?"

"What, honey?"

"Nothing. No chatter from the living room. No television and stereo in another part of the house. Just your heartbeat and mine."

"I'm sorry. I guess I'm just so used to it all I didn't realize how much it bothered you. In Boston we'll live in our own place and you can have your Pack medical practice if you want. Whatever you want."

She turned to him. "First I want to get out and go inside. And then, I don't want to talk about the Challenge or the Pack or anything but you and me for the next however many hours I have you. I want to pretend, just for a while, that we're normal."

"All right then. Come on, honey."

Inside, the house had been readied for them with candles everywhere. Grace lit the ones in the dining room and Cade turned on the stereo and Dave Brubeck filled the house. It was *normal.*

"Steaks for dinner. Let me get the grill started. You get a bath running for yourself. I did bring all your bath stuff. I didn't know which you'd like so I brought it all. I'll bring you a glass of wine in a bit."

She grabbed the bag and headed up the stairs where he'd indicated and into a bathroom the size of Texas with skylights and a sunken jetted tub. "Score." She turned on the water and lit the candles in there before shedding her clothes and pinning her hair up.

"Oh my favorite sort of wife. Naked and wet." Cade came in and placed a glass of wine on the ledge. "We've got a while before dinner. Any ideas on how to spend it?"

Cade's breath halted when she got to her knees, water cascading down her body and unzipped his pants.

"I have one or two, yes," she said before swirling her tongue around the head of his cock, making him nice and wet.

"I'm in complete agreement with this plan."

She shoved his pants down, one-handed, while gripping the root of him and holding him steady, taking him as deeply as she could.

Such a sight, her soft, smooth skin, beads of water glittering like diamonds in the candlelight as she sucked him into her mouth over and over.

"Damn it, you feel hot and wet. So good, Grace. That's it, yes." He groaned as he felt his body tighten. He had no resolve with her. The moment she touched him he neared climax. He'd never had such a powerful connection to anyone before. It might have been scary but instead, it was beautiful. *She* was beautiful.

She dipped her head down and tongued his balls. His head fell back. Her fist surrounded him, sliding up and down while she licked his sac.

Close. So close. He moaned and she moved up to the head, sucking him into her mouth hard and very wet. He thrust and came as he clenched his jaw and locked his knees.

One sweet kiss on the head, another on his belly. "That was lovely," she said, looking up at him.

He tossed his clothes and got into the bath, settling her on the edge and spreading her thighs wide. Waving his hand in the water, he used the sensation to slowly drive her up while licking and biting her nipples.

When she was sufficiently squeaky and practically shoved his head down to her pussy, he kissed his way down and buried his face there. Her clit, swollen and hard, bloomed against his tongue.

Her needy sounds buffeted him as he licked and tongued her, fucking into her with his fingers and playing against her ass. He'd take her there that night, when they were alone and relaxed, he'd be in every part of her before they went back home the next morning.

"Oh!"

He sucked her clit between his teeth, just barely grazing it. She jumped and then writhed. He bit the inside of her thigh and she shivered. The flat of his tongue pressed against her clit, swiping back and forth over her, time and again until the fingers sifting through his hair gripped him tight and held him there.

Her taste burst over his lips and tongue as she climaxed and then slowly slid into the water with a happy sigh.

He kissed her, lazy and slow. His taste mingled with hers and he wanted that moment forever.

Instead, he soaked there with her for a few minutes longer before getting out and putting his boxers on. “Going to go and get the steaks on.”

She smiled. “That was an excellent appetizer. I’ll be down to get some sides started in a minute.”

They worked in tandem. She in the kitchen and he alternated between the kitchen and the deck where the grill was. He knew they were being guarded. Lex had twenty wolves out there with laser sites and silver bullets. It gave him a sense of safety with her, the most precious thing in his universe.

After dinner, they washed up and headed back upstairs.

“So, Grace,” he whispered in her ear as he kneaded her shoulders and pushed his shirt off her shoulders. He loved that she wore them, loved her scent on his things.

“Mmmm?”

“Before you went to Chicago, I said I was going to take you here.” He slid his fingers over the curve of her ass and between. Grace jumped but then gentled again. Her breath was a bit shaky but he didn’t smell fear on her, only curiosity and desire. Good.

“I trust you. I want it. I want it because you do.”

There was simply nothing she could have said that would have turned him on more.

He laid her on the bed on her stomach and began to massage her, taking his time, kneading, caressing, touching. After a while, he put a bolster pillow under her hips, bringing her ass up. He’d already placed the lube nearby and poured some over her rear passage.

One hand worked her ass, slowly working his fingers in and the other found her pussy wet and ready. “Oh that’s it, honey.”

He brought the small vibrator out and turned it on. Putting it in her hand, he moved her so she could use it on her clit and into her gate. “Make yourself feel good. And relax. When I push in, bear down. Fuck yourself with the vibe when I take your ass, Grace.”

His voice shook as he slowly spread her enough to press the head of his cock against her and push inside. Just a bit, in and then out. Her body trembled but she was still with him.

Once he was all the way in, she slid the vibrator into her cunt and the vibrations wrapped around him.

“Not gonna last too long back here. You’re very tight. Hold on and it’s okay to come whenever you want, all right?” He’d leaned down to speak in her ear. He caught her scent, ridiculously ripe and turned on, and he nearly howled.

In and out he fucked, slowly, deeply and when she cried out and came, her entire body clamped down around him as she shoved back against him.

Mindless, he slid into her tight, smooth passage over and over until his orgasm grabbed his balls and didn’t let go.

Grace woke the next morning wrapped in a man, twisted in blankets. Her body ached but in a good way. He’d taken her so many times in so many ways she’d lost count. She was covered in love bites though, that made her smile even more.

He mumbled as she got out of bed and hit the shower. It was after nine, late for both of them, but it felt good. She’d needed the time with him, when he was all hers and it was just Grace and Cade. No Pack politics, no family stuff, no danger and no Challenge, just the two of them.

It had been the best gift she'd ever received.

He joined her some minutes later. "Coffee is on. We'll get breakfast and then we have to head back."

She tried not to frown. "Yum coffee. I'll make breakfast since you made dinner and midnight snack too."

"We'll have more time to ourselves. After."

"After breakfast you can start talking about it. I still own your ass. Although frankly I'm not up to doing much to it in a sexual nature. I'm a wee bit sore today."

The look on his face was of pure, masculine pride and she held back a smile.

She made pancakes and bacon while he'd scrambled eggs and they'd eaten as they sat close and held hands on and off.

True to his word, he didn't speak of anything of any import until they'd finished drying the dishes.

"We leave for Boston in two weeks. The location was chosen by a neutral third party. A Pack in Europe as a matter of fact. It's sealed, we just know it's in Boston, which makes sense because that's where National is headquartered. Bare knuckles, no weapons, to the death. He's already signed papers that attest that should he lose, all Pellini wolves surrender to National Allied Packs."

"And if you lose?"

Her voice shook. She hadn't meant it to. She didn't even want to mention it but she had to say it, had to know.

"Well, I won't. But if I do Pellini will challenge Lex for Cascadia lands. It's a huge risk, Grace. We could lose everything. But I won't lose. I don't even know why he made this Challenge and then poisoned Templeton. He has to know any of the top five Alphas would take him."

"He's messed up but he's not stupid. He has a plan and I

don't like it."

"What do you mean? You know him well, tell me what you think."

"He *wanted* the Challenge to be you and him. And the only way he can beat you without cheating, which will be closely monitored, is to infect you. That's his biggest weapon. He doesn't know you have all the stocks from before and he's got no idea I'm working on a vaccine. It's a risk, Cade. If he infects you and the vaccine doesn't work, you die. And then, I'll kill him. You need to understand that. I will violate the sanctity of that Challenge space and kill him."

He nodded. "Fair enough. But, your vaccine will work. I trust you. The truth is, I think you're right."

"Well, here's the thing, when he infects you, the virus will be active in your system for one minute. I'm trying to cut it down but that's my margin right now. You'll have the vaccine to render it inert. But he won't. Use that, Cade."

"Oh! Fuck, I hadn't thought of that. But that's poetic justice. Infecting him with what he tries to kill me with. And if he fights fair, I'll defeat him that way too. Good planning. I like how twisted you can be when you need it."

"I think you got quite a bit of that last night, didn't you?"

"Smartass. Let's go. You get working on that margin and I have to work on getting everything transferred over to Lex. Templeton and Carla are going to retire but he's offered to stay on as an Elder."

He helped her load her bags into the car and they drove back to the lab.

"Good. That will be useful. I want a house of my own. No one else living there. If you want to have guard houses next door and across the street and behind us, fine. If you want to buy a building and fill it with wolves, fine. But I want to be able to walk about naked and eat potato chips at two a.m. if I so desire."

"Your wish is my command. I'll have a realtor start looking, is that okay?"

She grinned. "I wish you were this agreeable about everything."

He laughed. "I am where it counts."

Chapter Eighteen

"This sucks." Nina adjusted herself in the seat as they made their way to Boston. Lex piloted the plane and Cade, the coward, left Grace to deal with her cranky sister-in-law.

"Drink some of the hot chocolate and stop whining."

"You know, that sweet thing is so just an act. I just want to go on record to say that now. You reel 'em all in with your big brown eyes and that teeny-tiny body and you're all cute and stuff. But scratch a layer and you're a bigger bitch than I am."

"Aww, Nina. I don't think that's possible." Grace fluttered her lashes and Megan burst out laughing.

"Ha. So funny. Now that you're abandoning me and I won't have a cool, fun baby doctor anymore and what I have a puppy instead of a pink, wrinkly thing? Huh? What then?"

"Was that even a complete sentence? The first one about me abandoning you? Because, if you recall, my ridiculous husband is going off to do some sort of cage match with my insane, homicidal brother. I'd rather be back in Seattle watching you eat eight of those tiny chocolate donuts at a time and scaring all the guards."

"They were already scared before Lex put me in a family way. And those donuts are Satan! I hate them, they leave a film on the roof of my mouth and yet I can't stop eating them. I blame you for that too. I don't quite know how it's your fault, but it is. Cade is just a big dumb wolf who's swinging his tool around. That's what they do. But you're supposed to be all higher brain functioning and stuff. I think his penis has brainwashed you or something." Nina moved around again, restless.

Grace pulled a pack of the cinnamon donuts from her bag and tossed them to Nina. "Here, crybaby, try those. And I now have a vision of Cade's penis in a tiny lab coat and a white Einstein wig as a mad penis scientist."

"Oh, these look good. Don't think so, Megan, get your own fetus that may or may not be a puppy and you can have your own donuts. Also, Grace, I will giggle when I see Cade and think of his penis. And that's your fault too. I hope you're happy."

Cade walked into the cabin and froze, blushing. "Um, do I even want to know what you're discussing?"

Grace waved at him, laughing. "Nothing unusual. Nina is telling us how she's thinking of your penis. But, as it makes her giggle, I'll let you, and her, live."

"Oh, Tiny, that's the first real laugh I've had since these dumb tools decided to take Warren up on the whole Challenge thing. And, these donuts are preferable to the chocolate ones. But if I have a puppy I'm gonna hunt you down."

Grace leaned over and touched Nina's knee. "I will be there when the baby comes. Unless you go very fast and early that is. I'll fly out before the due date and deliver her or him myself. I wouldn't miss that you know."

"Oh now you're going to make me cry." Nina shoved a donut into her mouth and Megan hugged her and handed her a handkerchief.

"We're nearly there, ladies. I came back to make sure you were all belted in and ready to land." Cade kissed Grace and she reached up to touch his face.

He took her hand and kissed her fingertips. "It's going to be all right."

Once he'd made sure everyone was belted in, he went back up with Lex, and Grace tried to force down her nervousness. But it lay in her gut along with the nausea she'd been feeling for the last week.

Cade held back, waiting for everyone to get off the plane so he could escort Grace himself. She held her back straight, he knew she wasn't feeling her best, chalked it up to worry. And yet, in her elegant black trousers and the blood-red blouse, she looked like a queen.

She took his hand and looked up at him. "I love you," she said before they left the plane.

They were blessedly alone for the moment and he dipped down to steal a kiss. "I love you too."

"Good. Because I'm pregnant. So you really can't die now."

He blinked and fell to his knees, putting his arms around her, burying his face in her chest. "Are you serious?"

She caressed his neck and he looked into her face. "Yeah. I found out this morning before we left. I had a feeling but I kept thinking that after the attack, I'd have lost it. But apparently not."

"Are you all right? Is the baby all right?"

"I'm fine. Nauseated but not too bad. I measured my hormone levels and they looked really good. I'll do some more tests but I have no reason to be worried."

"Holy shit, you're having our baby. You're so amazing."

"Meh, it's not that big a deal you know. Sperm meets egg, there you go." She grinned and he felt her joy through their bond.

"You're a miracle to me, Grace."

Her eyes filled with tears and her smile wobbled a bit. "I never thought I'd have anything like this, like you."

He stood, kissing her again and then laughing. "You do know that if you thought I was overprotective before, I'm going to be insufferable now?"

"It's another reason for you to win tomorrow, Cade. Now, come on, people are waiting."

He swept her up into his arms but the look of outrage on her face was enough to put her down before they hit the stairs to the tarmac of the small, private airport. "Sorry, got carried away."

"Wait until you get a room for that stuff, tough guy." Nina pretended to tap her toe. Cade just grinned. He wanted to share the news then but he knew it was better to share in relative privacy instead of in public.

"Good God, she did blow you didn't she?" Nina took in his look and Grace threw her hands up.

"Let's go, my fragile flower." Lex took Nina's arm and guided her to the waiting car while Cade and Grace, flanked by guards, did the same.

While she'd seen many werewolf females through pregnancy, Grace hadn't been prepared for the exhaustion of the first six weeks. She didn't have to worry like Nina did—natural wolves were a hearty bunch and even though it was difficult for many to get pregnant to begin with, once they were, problems were rare. Still, after four hours of endless protocol, she was ready to take a nap.

Cade looked at her after hour four had long passed and must have seen through her calm façade.

"I think it's time for a meal and some rest. Templeton, Carla, thank you for your hospitality." He stood and bowed deeply toward the retiring Alpha couple. Grace had been shocked to see how much older Templeton looked in the wake of his poisoning. He'd recover, but never quite regain his vitality as it had been before.

Her in-laws stood, along with Nina and Lex and a gazillion other Nationally Allied wolves, all in painstaking order of rank.

"We'll send a car for you in the morning. We won't know the location until half an hour before. You and Warren will be taken first, at sunup, to the site and sequestered until it's time for the Challenge. Representatives of the Argent Pack will handle all the details. You may each take one guard. As Lex will be taking your place as Alpha of Cascadia, I offer Jack, as he's your Enforcer once you take my place."

Jack stepped forward. "It would be my honor to stand as your guard, Cade."

Cade shook his hand. "Accepted. And Jack, I'm going to win so keep your paws off my wife." He winked but the words held an edge.

Part of the reason she'd told him that day instead of waiting until after the Challenge was male wolves grew even more protective and violent when their mates were pregnant. Which gave him even more of an edge in the ring tomorrow. She'd given him the vaccine the week before and she hoped like hell it would be all right. At that point, they didn't know exactly what Warren would have or even how Cade's system would synthesize the virus and vaccine when and if Warren used it. And he would, she was certain of it. But Cade would bite his ass and infect him and Grace wouldn't shed one damned tear for Warren.

After they finally escaped to Gabe's condo, Grace took her shoes off with a sigh.

"Sit your butt down, Grace. Dinner will be ready shortly, the whole family will be here and you'll need the energy. Can I tell them?"

He looked so sweet she couldn't have refused him anything. "Go on. I figured you would."

He practically skipped and she laughed. It didn't take long for Wardens by birth and their mates to begin to trail in. Layla and Sid, Tracy, Gabe and Nick were staying there with them so all they had to do was come downstairs. Beth and Henri were next door with Lex and Nina along with Megan. Dave was with Grace and Tegan entered with Ben.

"Wow this is some big gathering. Dang, Mom, you sure had a lot of kids." Lex winked at his mother who rolled her eyes.

"It'd be nice if it didn't take a Challenge to the death to get you all together like this. Now let's sit. Gabe's former personal assistant had this catered and it smells fabulous!" Beth shooed everyone to the huge table that'd been set out in the large dining area.

Before long, everyone was eating and chattering and Grace just watched the people who'd become her family. They all made her smile.

"Oh, so one thing I forgot to tell you all," Cade began and everyone quieted, turning to him. "Grace is pregnant." He turned to his mother, who was already crying. "You're going to have grandchildren coming out your ears, Mom."

"Just the way I like it." Beth put her hand on Grace's. "This is wonderful news. A good omen. I know their grandmother will agree." Cade's grandmother had a terrible fear of flying and they hadn't wanted to risk her taking a train so she was back in Seattle holding down the fort.

"How long have you known?" Nina asked, a huge smile on her face.

"Just since this morning. I had a feeling and so I did a few quick blood tests. I'll still come to deliver the baby. You're almost two months ahead of me so we'll be fine."

"Well it sucks that we can't be knocked up at the same time in the same house. Imagine the hormone-induced chaos we could have created."

"Yeah, gosh, I'll be sorry to miss that." Cade snorted and put another pork chop on Grace's plate. Her caloric intake would have to go way, way up so she just shrugged and started to eat it.

More pregnancy talk seemed to take the focus off the Challenge and in a way, Grace was glad. She really didn't want to think about it.

The family didn't stay overly late but there was a sense of expectancy. Everything was changing. After the Challenge, Cade would take on a huge new office, they'd move, Lex would ascend, babies, new houses, so much change, a lot of it good, especially the end of the war part.

Cade walked everyone out but asked Lex to wait. He and his brother went up to the roof garden and sat.

"If something happens to me tomorrow, I know you'll be able to hold Pellini off and keep Cascadia lands. But, look after Grace for me. She'll go to Jack, that's only normal and he'll do right by her. But my child, I want my child to know he or she is a Warden."

Lex looked up at the sky. "Of course."

"My will is in order. My belongings will go to Grace and I'm sure she'll make sure the family gets what it needs. I've deeded my share of the house to you and Nina. You'll find it in the desk drawer when you get back. Don't argue. It's a house you designed and you're the Alpha now."

Lex sighed, annoyed, but held his tongue.

"I love you and trust you with my life, my wife, my child, my Pack. You'll do me proud, you'll do Cascadia proud and there's no one I can imagine who'll lead better. Let Nina help, not like you'll have any choice in that. But she'll help you open the doors, modernize and make changes that'll better Cascadia."

"Cade, no one could ask for a better best friend, brother and Alpha than you've been. I'll be proud to watch you triumph tomorrow. Together we're going to lead wolves into a new world. Safer. More open. Don't hesitate tomorrow. No mercy, Cade. Because he has none and he will do whatever he has to, to win. If he tries to infect you, you bite him, do you hear me? Before you kill him, I want him to die knowing his fucked up handiwork is what ended him." Lex turned to him, vehemence in his features.

Cade nodded and together they went to find some sleep in the arms of their wives.

Grace lay in bed, her eyes drooping but still awake. When he came in she simply held her hand to him and he went.

Chapter Nineteen

Grace got up when he did. Stood with him as he shaved, scrubbed shampoo into his hair and washed his back.

She never looked from his face when he made love to her, the water pounding down on them both. He held her reverently, gently and yet, took what he needed and gave back in kind.

He pulled on loose-fitting pants, a long-sleeved shirt and sneakers and they waited for the escort together.

First Jack arrived, bringing coffee and bagels, something Grace appreciated even as her rioting emotions did not want her to eat.

"You'll wait and drive in with Templeton and Carla, understand? That's your place and you'll be safest. Be sure Dave never leaves your side." Cade kissed her when the escort arrived.

Dave, who'd been quietly reading the paper just across the room and giving them a bit of privacy simply nodded.

She wouldn't cry. She wanted to. She was scared for him. For them and the baby she carried. But he was strong and they had a secret weapon in the vaccine. Only Lex and Jack knew. Grace liked to believe Warren would find some way to fight fairly but she knew otherwise and had accepted that as she accepted his death.

"Be careful, Cade. I love you. I'll see you in a few hours and remember, if you die, I will be sorely pissed off and my pregnant butt will have to heave into the ring and kill Warren myself."

Jack jerked back and she realized they hadn't told him yet. She also realized that once they took Templeton's place, he'd be there just as Cade had with Lex and Nina. It would be a challenge but still, nice to know someone else she could count on was near.

"I promise. No dying. At least not me."

She watched as he left and Dave approached, hugging her and she let herself cry.

"Pregnant? You don't waste any time." Jack snorted. They'd been driven to a warehouse in South Boston. French wolves guarded the entire place with semi-automatic weapons and no-nonsense looks.

"It's the best damned thing I ever heard, Jack. My beautiful mate is carrying our child. She's amazing." Cade stretched and ate the meal they'd been provided. He'd need the calories and energy. Most likely he'd need to shift back and forth at least once and shifting took strength. He knew Warren would be taxed because he wasn't nearly as strong and nothing but birth, genetics or the position of your sire if you were made, created an Alpha. Warren Pellini was a strong wolf, but he wasn't an Alpha.

"You're a lucky man, Cade. Grace is everything a man would want in a mate. Smart, feminine, strong, brave and she adores you. Now, today you will kill this trash and walk away into a bright new future and I'll serve at your side. I hope I can do as well as Lex."

Cade laughed. "Lex will now have to deal with what a pain in the ass an Enforcer can be and I'll have to get used to problem solving with an Enforcer who won't think it's normal to get into a fist fight in the yard to resolve tension."

Jack grinned. "That's what you think. I have an older brother too."

"Grace is going to lose her mind with us," Cade said with a smile.

"She's little, but certainly a handful."

They small talked for the next hours as Cade tried not to think too hard and to just let his wolf take care of business. He was born to do it and he would. Hell, just to keep Jack from snapping Grace up if he died. But he wanted to see Grace's face every day until they both got very old and had great-grandchildren.

He knew when Grace entered the building. Her energy, calming and soothing even as she was anxious, filled their link.

"They're all filing in."

One of the French wolves came in and checked Cade over. It was bare knuckles, hand to hand and they provided him with a thin pair of tight-fitting shorts and watched him put them on.

"You ready?"

He took a deep breath. "As I'll ever be."

"Kick ass, take names and be my Alpha." Jack bowed low and let him pass.

Grace saw him walk out and his eyes immediately searched until they found her. Once they'd locked gazes, she relaxed a bit. He looked totally hot in next to nothing, all hard and muscled. She blew him a kiss and mouthed *I love you* and he grinned in return and put a hand over his heart as he bowed in her direction.

"Holy cow, he's like, a hunk!" Nina said. "Not like I'm

looking or anything." She snickered and Grace gave her the evil eye.

Lex took Grace's hand and she squeezed. Henri and Beth sat on her other side and her father-in-law took her other hand.

And then she saw her parents sit down on the other side of the roped-off fighting area. They wouldn't even look at her.

"Those your parents?" Lex asked quietly and she nodded. "They're going down after this. Are you all right with that?"

"They tried to have me killed. They've been aiding my brother in this whole insane biological warfare thing—yes, yes I'm all right with it."

Her father-in-law kissed her cheek. "You have real family now."

"You are both going to make me cry and I'll have to blame it on pregnancy hormones."

Lex laughed.

Warren entered. He'd lost some weight since she'd seen him last but even a stranger would have scented the fear pouring off him.

A wolf she didn't recognize but figured was the French envoy stood at the center of the ring. The gathered wolves shifted as the scent of bloodlust rose.

"The match will go on until one of the wolves in this ring is dead. Bare hands. The Challengers may transform back and forth between forms as many times as they are able. If anyone outside this ring seeks to intervene before the match is declared over, they will be executed by one of the numerous snipers up on the second floor. They are armed with silver shot."

Grace's heart sped as he walked out of the roped-off ring and Cade stood, easy and seemingly relaxed until the whistle blew and he immediately transformed and sprang at Warren.

Lex's hand tightened around hers but he stayed stock still otherwise, which gave her some confidence.

Warren's panicked face morphed into a wolf but much slower than would save him from the force of Cade's beast, from those razor-sharp teeth and nails.

A spray of scarlet arced through the air as Warren changed and they rolled a bit, teeth gnashing, the sound of flesh ripping, growling and yelping. Thank goodness she knew the sound of Cade's wolf and knew whose sound of pain it was.

It went on for the next ten minutes until Cade changed back again and jumped on Warren's back, wrapping his arm around Warren's throat.

And Warren changed, but it was slow. He struggled and that's when she saw him reach up and claw Cade.

Through their link, Grace knew instantly he'd been infected. "He did it," she hissed at Lex, who growled low and menacing.

Cade's system struggled and Grace counted time in her head. Cade staggered off and her eyes widened as he fell to his knees. Warren stood, a sneer on his face, thinking he'd gotten away with something. Grace held her breath, hoping he was wrong.

And suddenly, Cade's eyes cleared and he transformed into a wolf and leapt at Warren, catching him off guard and slicing his teeth into the other man's shoulder. Warren couldn't transform, he was already too tired and by the looks of it, the virus had taken over.

Cade slipped his fur and stood there, naked, furious and covered in blood and sweat as Warren fell.

His breath heaved as he and Warren held a long gaze, full of understanding. Cade wanted him to know what he died of. And then Cade moved to him, bent and snapped his neck.

The tears came then. Once she knew he'd live. Once she knew it was truly safe she opened up and began to weep, letting go of the fear she'd held for the weeks since the Challenge had been called.

The French envoy called the match and Warren's body was left there, disgraced, as Cade explained to them what had happened. For a wolf to cheat, especially after he'd already disgraced himself by violating the Palaver and was the reason for war, he'd pay the price. His body was carefully removed after Grace had a blood sample taken and put away. They'd take it, burn it and scatter it at the dump.

Her parents were taken into custody but she didn't bother to ask what would happen.

Cade had been surrounded by people since he'd been declared the winner and she needed him.

She pushed her way through and when she got to him, simply wrapped herself around his body and held on as he held her and finished up his business.

Cade saw her break, saw her weeping and relieved, watched his parents comfort her as Lex had moved down to the ring. He'd held everyone off until he stepped into the holding area and took a quick shower, wanting to get any potentially infected blood off his body.

The two brothers embraced but he'd still noticed Grace giving orders to get a blood sample from Warren's body. In fact, she'd looked over the corpse carefully even as Cade had answered questions about the virus and Warren's actions. Right as he'd finished, he noticed her removing something from his hands and slipping it into a bag.

God help him, he couldn't hide his reaction when she'd snapped off the latex gloves and tossed them into a garbage bag she'd then ordered Dave to be sure got burned.

And when she'd pushed her way through a throng of male wolves all well over six feet and grabbed him, he'd just held her, needing her as much as she'd needed him.

They'd gone back to Gabe's condo afterward. She'd really wanted to change into a track suit but put on a very nice dress instead, knowing she'd have to deal with werewolf politics.

Before that, she'd used the lab equipment Templeton had sent over and saw her suspicions were correct. She'd present the information that night when they went to the National Pack House.

She hadn't seen much of Cade since they'd returned. The War Council had met and were essentially wrapping up hostilities. Once the wolves associated with Warren had been exposed and shamed, they'd given up. Their lands and territory were even then being redistributed. Pack members would have the chance to swear fealty to the new governing Pack or leave, and Pellini Allied Pack leadership was being dealt with. Most would be shunned but some would face a worse fate. Grace decided not to think about that.

The war was over. Her baby would grow up in a world that was safe and she could do her job, go back to being a doctor and not have to be followed by ten wolves at all times.

"You okay, Grace?" Tracy asked her when she came downstairs. "Gabe just made sandwiches, here, sit."

"I wanted to thank you for letting us use your place." Grace sat. Gabe pushed a plate in front of her and she automatically began to eat.

"It was our pleasure to be able to give you shelter at such a time. You know, I understand you're looking for a place where you can live alone with Cade but have guards housed nearby. I own this building and I leased it to National. It would make us very happy to offer it to you and Cade."

"I think the bedroom right next to the master would be perfect for a nursery. It's secure, there's a guard station on the first floor and on the roof and the other guards could live here. Right now only two of the condos are occupied, one of them is Jack's. He moved in after we left for Portland." Tracy poured a huge glass of milk and gave it to Grace.

"Really?" Grace had been instantly enamored of the place. She'd loved the view, loved the sleek elegance of the building and the old world class of the neighborhood. It was plenty big, although it might be nice to take over the whole floor.

"I can see you're already planning." Gabe laughed. "I spoke to Cade and he said to bring it up to you. You two talk and we'll go from there."

Cade finally came in and moved straight to her, picking her up and kissing her as if he hadn't seen her for weeks. She held on, luxuriating in his taste, in knowing they had forever.

"Hi. That's a welcome."

He put her back down and nodded at the plates and everyone at the table.

"The war is over, boys and girls. Yellowstone, acting as the Pellini Allied representative, signed the agreement and I believe it's truly over."

"How are you feeling? Any lingering effects from the virus? I checked your blood, you show no traces at all of the virus." She'd breathed a sigh of relief at that. She'd held off on giving herself the vaccine when she'd inoculated Cade and now that she was pregnant she wanted to wait. But if he'd become a carrier it would have been a tricky thing.

"Fine. Better than fine. I still can't figure out how he infected me though."

“Ah! I can answer that.” She got up and went to the mini-lab she had set up in the downstairs office and brought back a vial.

“I was watching, it was when you transformed back that time and had your arm at his throat and were choking him. He scratched you. Do you remember? That’s when he infected you. You fell back right then.”

Cade thought for a moment and nodded. “Exactly. But he didn’t have any jewelry on and by that time he was naked. And he wasn’t infected because when I bit him he got infected and was dying when I snapped his neck.”

She gently shook the vial and it made a gentle clinking sound. “He had this under one of his fingernails. A small injector, with a reservoir in it. It had been imbedded in his nail bed which is why it stayed when he took his wolf and then changed again. All he had to do was hit it just right and it would have released the virus through the needle. He appeared to scratch you and then he jumped back. He was waiting for you to die but not getting close enough for you to grab at him. You surprised him when you transformed like that.”

“That’s some heavy duty spy type shit,” Gabe said and she nodded.

“That’s exactly the kind of place you’d expect to see this sort of thing.”

“Are you okay?” Cade asked her. “We need to go to the Pack House. If you’re okay with me taking over as Supreme Alpha that is. You know, Templeton can stay on and I’m sure Lex will let me have my old job back.”

“I told you a week ago, and a week before that, and before that, I accept it. My place is beside you in all things, Cade. If fate means for us to lead here, we’ll do it. And our child will come into a world we’ve made better.”

"I'm so lucky." He kissed her again.

"You are. Now let's go."

The streets around the Pack House were filled with cars and inside it was wall-to-wall werewolves. When Cade and Grace entered, all heads bowed and then applause and howls broke out.

Templeton, with his wife Carla at his right and Jack at his left, waited for them in the main living room.

"Are you ready, Cade Warden? Are you ready for the leadership of the wolves on this land to fall to you and your mate?" Templeton asked.

"I give all I have and all I am to my wolves." Cade got to his knees.

"I give all I have and all I am to my wolves." Grace followed.

Templeton sliced his palm with a sharp knife. The metallic scent of blood filled the air. Carla took the knife and did the same. Their mixed blood hit a small chalice of earth, symbolic of the nation of wolves.

They stepped back. "We've given ourselves and now fade away so that a new Alpha may reign."

Cade helped Grace up and sliced his hand open and Grace followed. Their blood hit that same earth and the magic of that action, the magic of their intent crackled through the room and suddenly she felt it. Felt the lives of wolves for miles and miles.

At first it was frightening but slowly, as Cade held her with one arm around her shoulders, it settled into place.

"I feel my nation and I take them as my own. May I always do honor as their leader."

Grace repeated the words and it was over.

The party went on into the very late hours of the night until Carla tucked Grace up into one of the spare bedrooms in the Pack house. Dave settled in a chair nearby. He'd decided to come to Boston with them to stay as her guard. Megan would be the new Enforcer of Cascadia.

Cade came in as the sun rose and woke Dave. Cade carried his sleeping mate to the car and they drove back to the condo. Tracy and her men had gone back to Portland and the place was all theirs. Dave took the place just across the hall and a full guard regiment passed from Templeton to them and were in place in the office downstairs and would be twenty-four hours a day. Monitors, movement sensitive alarms and sniper positions would guard them and keep them safe.

Epilogue

A year later

"Hurry up! She's asleep and I'm so horny I'm going to die if you don't touch me."

Cade closed the door to Becca's room and tossed his clothes as he approached his very beautiful and demanding wife.

"Naked and horny, my favorite combination."

She laughed and opened her arms. And he went where he belonged.

Her hair had gotten longer and he freed it from the loose braid. It fell down around her face and shoulders like fine silk, her scent hitting him in a way only she had the power to.

He kissed her. Took her mouth, owned her, possessed her and feasted. Teeth and lips, tongue against hers as her gentleness made way for his ferocity. She gave him what he needed, her hands held his head, keeping him in the kiss until he was drunk with it.

She pushed and rolled him, straddling his body.

"I can't wait. I don't want to wait."

"I wanted to go down on you," he said in a growl.

"You can later, after."

He let her have her way with him, watching the sweet line of her body as she reached around and grabbed his cock and thrust herself down on it.

Sensation rushed through him, nearly blinding him as the tight, hot silk of her cunt gripped him.

"That never fails to feel so fucking good I think I may die." He caressed up the curve of her hips, over the flat again belly, even just months after Becca's birth. She'd joked about wanting to find a way to bottle werewolf metabolism and make a billion dollars. But he'd loved her body when she'd been heavy with their daughter as much as he loved it now.

He found her breasts, marveling at their shape and sensitivity as he always did.

She made the sounds that drove him wild as she began to ride his cock, her nails slightly digging into his ribs as she held on.

He fell into their link, lazing through the heady pleasure they both felt. Even tired, he wanted her every moment. He wasn't going to rush through now that they had the time alone.

She dragged it out, keeping her rhythm slow and steady.

"You're the most beautiful thing I've ever seen, Grace. You make every day worth living."

Her eyes, glazed with pleasure, cleared as she looked down into his face with a surprised, but pleased smile. "Cade, I love you. I don't think I even had much of a life before you came into it."

He slid a hand between them and found her clit, brushing his fingertip over it slowly, just a feather-light touch.

Her body tightened slowly as he drew closer and closer. When she came, he held back so he could watch the transformation of her features. "So gorgeous when you come around my cock."

"Now you," she gasped.

And after he came and had laid her down, he spent long minutes kissing her. Taking her lips and across her jaw. She arched and he took the invitation to kiss down her beautiful neck and over her collarbone, stopping to feast on the hollow of her throat. Her breasts, the nipple and the enticing curve below beckoned as did each rib, the hollow of her belly, the rise of each hip bone—all drew his lips, all gave him a different taste of his wife, his woman.

He coaxed her with whispers and caresses and her thighs parted. Pressing his lips at the hollow behind each knee, he moved to her center, opened the folds of her pretty pink pussy up and gazed. Feasted his eyes on the part of her that'd sheltered him half an hour before.

Long slow licks, he took her slow and with great care. He tasted every part of her cunt, the line of each curve and dip, loving her responses.

She came in a hot rush, and afterward, he simply rested with his head on her thigh as she sifted her fingers through his hair in that calming way only she had and he closed his eyes against the overwhelming goodness of that very moment. His wife in his bed, his child in the room next door and his people all thriving.

About the Author

To learn more about Lauren Dane, please visit www.laurendane.com. Send an email to Lauren at laurendane@laurendane.com or stop by her message board to join in the fun with other readers as well. www.laurendane.com/messageboard

Marc must face the biggest challenge of his life—convincing Liv Davis that he means to love her forever.

Chased

© 2007 Lauren Dane

Book Three in the Chase Brothers Series

Liv Davis had just about given up on her happily ever after. Burned by love more than once, she's beginning to think Mr. Right wasn't in the cards for her.

Marc Chase is a confirmed bachelor and lover of women—lots of them. He's determined not to fall head over heels the way his brothers have. Until he kisses Olivia Davis and realizes head over heels may not be such a bad thing after all!

Can Liv open her scarred heart for this younger ladies man? She loves Marc more than she can begin to admit but she's terrified of being rejected again. Marc faces a challenge greater than he's ever faced before. Making a woman believe he's more than just a great bedmate—making her believe he's in it for good.

In the end it will all come down to two days in a hotel and a bet. Can they both win?

Available now in ebook and print from Samhain Publishing.

Enjoy the following excerpt from Chased...

Marc's place smelled like his cologne and fresh fruit. She saw a set of hanging baskets filled with apples and peaches and knew that's where the scent had come from. His living room windows were large and looked out over the street. It was nicely furnished with bookshelves on the walls and pictures of his family all around.

He kept surprising her and that made her uncomfortable. In the box marked *unavailable bachelor for life*, he was non-threatening because it wouldn't pay to develop feelings for him. But in the box labeled guy way deeper than she'd thought who loved his family? That guy was dangerous to her well being.

"Now." He flipped the lights off before lighting candles set all around the living room. "I'll be right back." He disappeared down the hall, returning after a few moments. "You look gorgeous with candlelight on your skin. I figured you would. Then again, I've yet to see you in a situation where you didn't look gorgeous."

His hands went to the tie at the right shoulder of her shirt and undid it, letting it fall forward. Her nipples, already hard at his presence, hardened even more at the cool air and the look on his face.

"Okay, let's go down the hall before I take you here on the floor of my living room. I've already had you in a truck, I need to mind my manners now."

She laughed and let him drag her down his hallway to his bedroom. A king sized bed dominated the space.

"I've been dreaming of this," he murmured, pulling his shirt up and over his head. Her heart raced at the sight of him, tawny in the candlelight.

"God you're beautiful."

He stopped and cocked his head, smiling. "Thank you, sugar. I've got nothing on you."

Her blouse lay around her waist and she removed it, laying it on the arm of a chair.

"Nothing on me." She snorted. "Puhleeze. Look at yourself in that mirror there. You're gorgeous. Hard and fit and muscular. I know you know you're handsome, women fall over you all the time and you catch quite a few too."

Chuckling, he unzipped her pants and shoved them down, letting her lean on him as she stepped out of them and her shoes.

"Good gracious." He stalked around her, taking in every inch of her body. A body he'd helped her shape and strengthen. She'd never been ashamed of her nudity but she certainly felt a lot better about her overall tone and shape now that he'd kicked her ass for two and a half months.

"Now you. I want to see all of you."

He stopped in front of her and slowly undid the buttons at the front of his jeans. Each *pop* of the seven buttons drew her nerves, and her nipples, tighter.

He shoved his jeans down and off his body, taking his socks off with them and then stood gloriously naked in front of her.

"Wow." Her mouth dried up. Flat, hard stomach with an enchanting line of hair leading to his very healthy equipment. Listing to the left. She liked that, liked how it'd felt inside her. Right then it was very hard. "I do so love a man with such a good recovery time."

He laughed but made no move to stop her as she took her time looking him over, taking in every inch of his body. Unable to stop herself, she skimmed her palms down his back and over his muscled ass. "This is even nicer unclothed."

When she reached his front again, his eyes were a deep, dark green and a very naughty grin had taken residence on his lips. A thrill worked through her at the sight of that face. Shit, she totally should have started doing younger men years ago. Even as she thought it, she knew it was a lie. It wasn't about his relative youth, it was about *him*.

"By the way? You're not overcompensating. Not at all."

Surprise overtook his features for a moment and he threw his head back to laugh. The floor swept out beneath her and she landed with a laugh on the bed, Marc looming over her.

"Did you like what you saw?"

"I like what I see very much. I'd like it even more if you got busy with all those arms and legs, your mouth and hands and that verra fine cock you've got there."

"On your hands and knees then. Face the other way. I want to fuck you from behind but this way I can see your face in the mirror. See you come with those beautiful cat eyes looking up at me so you don't forget who's bringing you such pleasure."

Holy shit, the man was lethal with the talking. Who knew? Ugh, again with the surprises. He was like the ultimate Pandora's box of naughty.

She moved quickly and he settled himself behind her. They were well matched height wise, his groin pressed against her ass and the back of her pussy.

But he didn't plunge in. Instead he bent and licked the length of her spine until a soft squeal of surprised pleasure came from her.

"I don't have any neighbors and the shoe store is closed. Feel free to make as much noise as you like." The edge of his teeth found her hip, biting her gently. "I just want to eat you up." He paused and met her eyes in the mirror. "Again."

She moaned as shivers of delight broke over her. She looked back, under the line of her body, watching as he sheathed himself.

"Now then." He pressed the head of his cock just inside her body and waited. One of his hands gripped her hip, keeping her from ramming herself back against him to take him inside. The other stole around her body and palmed a breast, moving to slowly tug and roll the nipple until she writhed as much as she could.

"Please!"

"Please what? Tell me what you want, Liv."

"Fuck me. Please. Stop teasing me and fuck me."

"My pleasure." He slid deeply into her in one strong push before pulling out nearly all the way.

If Marc hadn't already loved her, watching her as he fucked her would have sealed the deal. It took a lot of trust for a woman to let herself be taken from behind like that. More trust to tell a man what she wanted and then to receive it with utter erotic abandon.

Her breasts swayed as she moved back to meet his thrusts, soft sounds broke from her as he played with her incredibly sensitive nipples. She was wet and creamy and he'd never felt anything as good as being deep inside her. His fingertips found her clit again, coaxing her into another orgasm.

And when she came? Holy moley she looked absolutely luscious. Her face flushed, eyes glassy, lips wet from her tongue. He'd seen a lot of women orgasm, but this one was beyond compare.

He loved how easy it was to make her climax as well. Once when he'd gone down on her, another as he made love to her in the truck, a third time with his hands just moments before and now he'd have her do it herself.

Printed in the United States
143475LV00004B/1/P

9 781605 040950